THE

WAITING

ROOM

Also by Diane Eklund-Āboliņš

An Ambiguous Tragedy
45 Days: Walking the Bibbulmun Track
Room Nineteen
The Space in Between: A Story about Nina

Poetry
On the Circle
Glänsande vitt på blått

THE
WAITING
ROOM

Diane Eklund-Āboliņš

First published in Australia in
2019
by
AoE Publishing
Sydney, Australia

ISBN: 978-0-9873473-8-1

"There are things known and things unknown, and in between are the doors of perception." Aldous Huxley

ARTHUR

The waiting room, which to some may seem quite large and to others relatively small, is a medium-sized rectangular room with cream walls, burnt-orange doors, and light-coloured bamboo flooring. It can, however, appear either rectangular or square, depending on both the perspective and emotional state of the person entering it. The floor can vary from dark polished timber to an uninteresting cheap beige linoleum, and the colour of the walls fluctuates, depending again on the individual, between off-white, old rose, and midnight blue. However, no matter their perspective regarding the size and colour of the room, everyone agrees that there are no windows and only two doors.

The room is entered from the end of a long and relatively wide corridor lit with overly bright fluorescent lights; after entering the room, it can be seen that the entry door is positioned two-thirds to the left. Beyond this door and close to the left wall of the room there is a laminate reception desk that is not much more than a long table, with a black leather swivel chair behind it. Not everyone will perceive the table as being long or even laminate, and they may decide that it is constructed of some kind of timber, or plastic, or even opaque glass. At the same time, there will be those who claim that the chair is blue and padded while others might argue that it is definitely not a swivel chair.

There is nothing on the desk except for two neat piles of white A6 paper - one considerably larger than the other - and an expensive-looking black ballpoint pen with gold trim. The desk itself is behind, and slightly left of, two loosely formed rows of cheap aqua-coloured plastic chairs. No matter the many varying individual perceptions of the room, no one is able to ignore the fact that the chairs are both aqua and plastic, and that all the chairs are facing away from the entry door towards the front of the room. In the very centre of the front wall is the second door.

There is an irregular trickle of people entering through the first door: a couple of people, a break, another person; and then, after a much longer break when it might be easy to imagine that no one else will be coming, another person. Throughout the long afternoon, the pattern continues to

3

repeat itself with longer or shorter breaks and fewer or more people.

On entering the room, most people tend to look around with expressions varying from surprise or irritation to obvious deep concern, before, catching sight of the reception desk on their left, they move either hesitantly or resolutely in that direction.

The receptionist – an angular, unattractive woman in her fifties with short grey hair and red-lacquered nails – is fully engrossed either in her Personal Screen or in her knitting, and she shows not the least amount of interest in the person standing on the other side of her desk. Whether it could be called a positive or a negative trait, her disinterest is consistent, and everyone is treated with the same lack of emotion and communication. In most cases, she makes the person wait while she very slowly finishes the page she is reading on her PS or the row she is knitting. She then removes her eyes from her Personal Screen or places her knitting carefully on the desk, skims the letter handed to her by the person in front of her, writes the person's number on one of the pieces of paper on the desk, moves it to the smaller of the two piles, and points at the two rows of plastic chairs.

Most people, after a moment of bewildered uncertainty, cautiously make their way towards the uncomfortable-looking chairs and, choosing one, sit down. Some people hesitate before moving away from the desk, looking as though they want to raise their voices to ask questions or to complain, but most of them think better of it, keep their mouths closed, and say nothing. Occasionally, someone does say something, but it is never to any avail, as, by that point, the receptionist has already retreated into her knitting or the words flickering on her screen and is no longer contactable. Apart from the occasional hushed conversation, the only sounds that can be heard are the regular, muted sound made by the large white electric clock on the wall behind the reception desk, the irritating clicking sound of the receptionist's knitting needles, and the infrequent sharp, discordant sound of chairs scraping on the floor as people try to find more comfortable positions.

While they wait.

And wait.

And wait.

Arthur - tall, mid-thirties, brown hair, blue eyes, intelligent-looking, well-dressed, and wearing steel-rimmed glasses - has chosen a chair at the end of the second row of eight or ten well-spaced chairs, furthest from the receptionist's desk. He did so, knowing that it would give him a view of practically everyone in the room, including the receptionist. He likes to at least *feel* that he is in control, and sitting where he can see everyone gives him the only smidgen of control available to him in his present situation.

His perspective regarding the room is that it is a relatively large rectangle with a polished timber floor and white walls. The receptionist's desk is also made from timber, and the chair is definitely a swivel chair, and it is grey-blue.

While he is reflecting on the appearance of the room, he is still not sure why he is there. For Arthur, the word *waiting room* has always conjured up images of medical and dental surgeries, law companies, and school offices. He accepts the fact that police stations, as well as train and bus stations, also have waiting rooms, but these are not the images that he equates with the word. A waiting room for Arthur is a room that leads to another room, which is completely hidden from view; a room where something happens - the something for which one is waiting.

He has a deep fear and a distrust of anything connected with Building C, and he assumes that this is the case for most people: he cannot imagine that it would be otherwise. He has spent the last few hours asking himself why he would have been sent a letter requesting his presence there at a certain time on a certain date. The letter did not specify any reason for his being called to Building C, which Arthur finds extremely troubling. He racks his brain, but he cannot remember having done or said anything inadvertently, and he certainly has not made any appointments that would require a waiting room. Or has he? The whole experience has made him more unsure of himself than usual. Perhaps he made a doctor's appointment, and then he forgot, or perhaps he *did* do something that he should not have done or said something that he should not have said. His brain is working overtime, trying to decipher the puzzle.

On the other hand, he is very aware that if he thinks too hard, too deeply, or too long, he may finally discover the answer, and this possibility also frightens him. He could probably cope with remembering that forgotten medical or dental appointment - he would be happy to know that the reason for the letter was so simple and ordinary - but does he really want to know that he has been called to the room for a completely different reason? He cannot make up his mind, so he vacillates between trying to work out why he has been called to Building C and trying to wipe the whole dilemma from his mind.

He is conscious of his inability to quickly and easily make up his mind about anything and everything, and he worries incessantly that he may make the wrong choice or that he may say the wrong thing in the wrong situation at the wrong time. He knows that he has already made lots of wrong choices, though some of them have not been especially important, like choosing to walk down one street in preference to another and then discovering that the street of choice is a dead end; or, after much thought and deliberation, selecting the bag of apples with the rotten apple at the bottom. Some choices, however, have been life-changing: he still cannot understand why things went so wrong with Rowena all those years ago. In spite of, or perhaps because of, his indecision and worrying, Arthur spends a lot of time noticing things, both big and little things, probably more than most other people. He is quite sure that life must be much easier for everyone else.

It all began with the letter he received ten days ago. Letters are very past tense: no one writes letters any longer; in fact, there is no longer a postal service. Writing letters went out of vogue two or three decades back, and, now, any letter that arrives in any letterbox has been sent by Administration and has been delivered by the Administration's own delivery service. Initially, a good twenty years past and before the advent of the PS, Administration sent all important notifications to each person's phone (which, it could be argued, was somewhat similar to the PS but without all the present features and extras). When people received these notifications many of them pressed the delete button without even so much as looking at what they were deleting, while others simply lost the notifications amid all the other communications - most of them reminders about the great job Administration was doing. Administration decided that a concrete message in the form of a physical letter probably made more sense. Perhaps when people were able to hold a letter in their hands they would be more aware of the importance of the notification; moreover, the letter was always tangible confirmation that the information had, in actual fact, been sent.

When Arthur retrieved the letter from his mustard-yellow letterbox - third row of ten, fifth from the right, one of the many letterboxes set into the wall at the front of his building - he did not have to wonder who had sent it. Letterboxes, like letters, were outdated and unnecessary, but Administration needed them to send official communications, so everyone had to have a letterbox. If people were honest, most of them wanted the letterboxes made redundant; no one felt comfortable with the thought that Administration was constantly looking over their shoulder, checking their every move, commenting on everything they had done, should have done, or should not have done.

As expected, the envelope was mid grey and rectangular - all official letters were placed in mid grey rectangular envelopes - and he held it gingerly in one hand as he walked to the lift. He would have liked to have been able to drop it into a waste disposal unit, if such a thing had been at hand, but if one had been available, and if he were to do such thing, how would he later explain his action to Administration? He wished that he had never received the letter: he did not want anything in his life to change. He desperately wanted everything to remain as it had been before he opened his letterbox. Not that everything was great, not by any means, but he had a gnawing feeling in his stomach that opening the letter would somehow draw a line between what had been - no matter whether it was good, bad, or indifferent - and what was about to be, and he was not sure that he really wanted to be pushed across such a line.

Back inside his small flat on the third floor of the relatively new orange concrete building that was more or less identical to the other orange or grey or white or yellow twenty- and thirty-storey buildings in his area, he had placed the envelope, unopened, on the bench above his kitchen table, pretending that it did not exist, that it never *had* existed. Had he dared, he would have thrown it away - he had a waste disposal unit beneath his kitchen sink - but to take such a step would signify that he both acknowledged and confirmed its existence and, armed with such knowledge, he had then wilfully made a decision to obliterate the evidence. In spite of his dislike for the envelope, and whatever was inside of it, he was not brave enough to consider obliteration and all the possible consequences.

The envelope sat on the shelf for more than a week, glowering down on him while he ate breakfast and dinner and, on the weekend, lunch. If the envelope had been able to open itself, it probably would have done so. Arthur tried not to think of it, but his eyes would often wander to the shelf of their own accord, and finally he decided that he had no option: until he was prepared to confront that invisible, but very definite, line, his life was going to remain like a still from some film. In the end, his curiosity, mixed as it were with a sense of foreboding doom, got the better of him: he opened the letter.

Inside the mid-grey rectangular envelope there was one piece of reasonably stiff, pale grey paper with several lines of electronically printed text. At the bottom of the page there was a hard-to-read signature and an official-looking round stamp. As he stood in his kitchen with the paper in his hand, he did not doubt that he had already crossed the line between then and now and that his past had been relegated to some blurry place where memory was no longer reliable. Everything he could see in front of him suddenly took the form of a very large, out-of-focus question mark.

His eyes moved quickly over the text. He had to read it several times, because he knew that it was that invisible line between what was and what was about be: he was being told that he was to go to Building C on the sixteenth day of the month. He automatically looked at the calendar hanging on the wall near the door. A coldness descended over him as he realized that the day's date and the date on the letter were one and the same. He looked back at the letter, his eyes moving frantically along the lines of confident black characters parading against the soft grey background. 'Present yourself at reception on the thirty-sixth floor of Building C at 14.00 on the sixteenth day of this month. Bring nothing with you.'

There was no other information. The letter gave no indication as to why he had been called to Building C, one of the main government buildings, which housed departments as disparate as health and wellness, taxation, and criminal justice. It could be something as benign as a regular health check, or it could be something much more ominous.

Having finally crossed the line, he was anxious, angry, and annoyed, but as he sat at his kitchen table he knew that he had no choice. The alternative - not presenting himself at reception on the thirty-sixth floor of Building C at 14.00 - simply did not bear thinking about.

Arthur sighs deeply and crosses and then uncrosses his legs. He has been sitting on the hard, uncomfortable chair for almost two hours, and he desperately wants to be able to stand up and stretch himself. Even though every minute cell in his body is on the point of screaming, he does not want to do anything that would draw undue attention to himself. No one else is standing up and stretching.

If he had been anyone else other than himself he might have struck up a conversation with person on his left, a portly middle-aged man with a significant bald patch surrounded by thinning, grey hair; but Arthur is far too introverted to launch into unnecessary small talk with a stranger. Parallel with all of this physical and mental discomfort, he is thinking that it should be the reception-ist's business to explain to him why he has been called to the waiting room in the first place, but that does not appear to be part of her job description.

When he first arrived he did ask her what the appointment was for. Was it a dental appointment he had somehow managed to forget or was it the yearly medical? Thinking back he was sure that his question was polite, low-key, and, given the situation, relatively pleasant, but the receptionist had merely looked straight through him and said nothing. When she made no reply he had wondered if perhaps she was hard of hearing, and he had been on the point of repeating himself when she said coldly:

'That will be all, 7891-447; you may take a seat.'

It does not occur to him that other people may see the room differently, in the same way that it does not occur to him that some people may have a completely different understanding of both the letter and the reason why they have been called to the waiting room. Although it is not something that is currently at the forefront of his thought processes, he has always been aware that interpretations of anything can vary, depending on the person, the situation, and the perspective.

He has never liked waiting rooms, even though his dislike is probably not so much of the waiting room itself but of what is beyond the room: the thing for which one is waiting. His mind circles around childhood visits to the dentist, always in the company of his father. For some reason his mother is not part of the memory, though it was very likely she had been there, and he has simply forgotten. He has, however, not forgotten the waiting room itself: a stuffy square-shaped room with one small, rather grimy, window looking out on to a busy street three floors below. There had been a low, brown table in the middle of the room, and in his memory it is always untidily covered with outdated, tired-looking magazines. Thinking back, he wonders if there may have been a time, perhaps early in the morning, when all the magazines were gathered into neat, evenly placed piles. While he is still thinking about the table and the piles of reading matter, his mind zooms in on the drooping green plant with the sickly yellow tinge, silently crying out for water as it stands in its huge white ceramic pot near the door; the five or six mismatched chairs; a dull, grey linoleum floor with several worn patches; and the off-white door leading to the dentist's surgery - the unavoidable reality for which everyone is waiting. There may have been a desk with a receptionist, but he can no longer remember it, as any such image has well and truly receded into a shadowy darkness where all unwanted images go to hide.

Although the desk and the dental receptionist may have completely disappeared, he can clearly see himself, sitting on the edge of the high-backed wooden chair, his hands held like blinkers on each side of his head as he moves it in an irregular circle, his eyes noting the table, the plant, the other chairs, the surgery door, and then the window, before making the same journey again but in the opposite direction. Without dwelling on the memory, he knows that it never took long before his father would reach across and, placing his hand firmly on his shoulder, say: 'That's quite enough now, son.'

There were nearly always other people in the waiting room: those who sat quietly, but anxiously, on the dissimilar chairs, and children whose eyes never left the fascinating, yet horrifying, almost-white door. Now, forcing his thoughts back over the years, he searches for words to describe the atmosphere in the room, and his mind decides that it was *tight, tense,* and *suffocating.* So many years later, he can still call to mind the traffic sounds from the street below, sounds that now twist and turn around the memory of *tight, tense,* and *suffocating.*

The atmosphere in his current waiting room is also tight, tense and suffocating.

While his mind is forcing him to relive the unpleasant, constricting atmosphere and the jarring sounds, he is fully aware that the obsessive-compulsive manner in which, as a child, he had observed everything and everyone in the waiting room had simply been his way of quelling the anxiety inside of him. The awareness brings him back to his present situation with a start: he is more than certain that he could benefit from some kind of ordered, repetitive brain activity to focus his thoughts and tone down the reality around him. He may have hoped that a mindless routine would help dampen his present anxiety, but moving his eyes up and down the two rows of aqua-coloured chairs and around the people seated on them is not helping, and he is unable to think of anything else he could do instead.

Arthur has created many routines to help him cope with life and the precariousness of choice. As a child in a dentist's waiting room he was locked into someone else's decision, and he is still not sure what is worse - making the wrong choice or having to accept a choice that someone else has made. He is very aware that things are never as simple as he would like them to be, but he does what he can to make his life more bearable. His routines, most of them unexplainable even to himself, have a veneer of some ritualistic act, and in many ways they are not unlike the chants and mystifying actions of the witch doctor or even the religious practitioner. Each routine comes with its own boundaries and set of rules that make Arthur feel secure and safe; without his routines he would be rudderless, and he would most possibly flounder and finally drown.

Rowena had said that she was only trying to help him. She wanted him to see a psychologist - she even made an appointment for him - but Arthur could never understand her reasoning. He had tried psychologists and counsellors before, and he had come to the conclusion that he did not need their help; he was managing particularly well. What would a psychologist do other than remove all his routines and rituals, and where would he be then? Everyone had their rituals, he argued; they were simply part of life. When he ordered things in the kitchen or the bathroom according to a special set of rules, based on size or colour or ingredients or shape, it was not an indication that he needed help - far from it - it was confirmation that he was in tune with the natural forces around him. He was living in harmony with life itself.

Eventually Rowena offered him an ultimatum: either he accept the fact that he needed professional help and see a psychologist or else she was going to leave him. She loved him, but he was driving her insane. Arthur had no intention of seeing a psychologist, so Rowena packed her things and moved out of his house. Looking back on it years later, in a moment of unusual clarity and honesty, Arthur admitted to himself that it was he who had instigated the break-up - he could have *seen* the psychologist; he need not have followed his advice. He still missed Rowena, and he often wondered where she was now and what had become of her.

It is undeniable that the terrifying thing about all waiting rooms is the unknown factor beyond the actual waiting room. After all, the very name *waiting room* signifies something apart from the activity of waiting: people are waiting, but waiting for what? he wonders. Whenever there is a waiting room, there is always a wall and a door, or some other kind of division, separating the now from the then. The *then* remains invisible and unknown until one passes from the waiting room to—

His train of thought abruptly stops, and he moves his weight on his chair, stretches his legs, and, for some reason that not even he understands, directs his gaze to the back of the head of the person sitting in front of him - a man with dark, curly hair, which, Arthur reflects, is long overdue for a cut. Small white flecks of dandruff decorate the collar of the man's coat.

Arthur looks away, more than slightly disgusted, and automatically sweeps his hand over his trouser legs several times. Not that the man is sitting so close that any of the dry skin particles could have drifted so far, but Arthur is taking no chances. He brushes his trousers yet again; if he could surreptitiously move his chair back a little he would do so.

He tries to block out the unpleasant reality that is in front of him while his mind fumbles with other thoughts that are beginning to run awry. While he is still thinking about white flecks on collars and trousers, he also thinks: is life about anything else but waiting? From the very moment we are born we find ourselves in a kind of undefined waiting room, waiting for the end – an end that has to come, though we do not know when. Then, suddenly, the image of life as one enormous waiting room splits off into countless small waiting rooms with doors leading to spaces where there are even more waiting rooms. Waiting is clearly what life is all about: he finds himself wondering if there is actually anything else.

His thoughts move to what might be behind the door. First he imagines a small room, not dissimilar to the dentist's surgery of long ago; then for no explainable reason he pictures a very large open space, which incorporates a large portion of floor thirty-six. In this room or space there are no room dividers, no furniture - nothing. Looking across the area, which has some resemblance to the floor of a warehouse, he can see windows, and equating windows with everything that is beyond the walls of the building he thinks of freedom and all the things he believes he is missing at the moment. The image of the large open-plan room ripples, begins to fade and almost turns into another image, but Arthur is interested in what it might be able to tell him, and he grabs hold of it and brings it back into his consciousness.

He can see that it is dark outside, though he is aware of many abstract patterns of light emanating from other buildings. The light in the room itself is muted and subdued and does not distract from all the other external lights. After the bright light of the waiting room it is something of a relief. In his mind, Arthur walks slowly towards the windows, wondering at the vastness and the total emptiness of the space. Without saying anything, he wonders: What is it used for? Why is it empty? Why is it connected to the waiting room? Even though the room with its windows and empty space is all a figment of his imagination, he thinks: if this is what we are waiting for then nothing makes any sense.

The windows - long, slim rectangles placed at intervals of roughly two metres - reach from the floor almost to the ceiling. In the soft light of the room against the dark outside they appear as columns, holding the space together, protecting it.

He crosses the room and stands at one of the windows. He looks down and then up. It is dark, and his vision is somewhat limited, but he is able to see that there is nothing below him and nothing above him: floor thirty-six is hanging, unsupported, somewhere between heaven and earth.

He wonders why he should be thinking about a room hanging in a piece of dark space. The imagery worries him: some kind of connection with the ground is always important unless one is on a plane. But a plane never hangs, it is always en route to a destination, and it will eventually land. A room simply hanging between heaven and earth is not en route anywhere: it is static. Worryingly static.

He wonders if the image is trying to tell him something: perhaps his life is static; perhaps *he* is static? His mind circles the word static: lacking in movement, action, or change. Yes, that would probably describe him; when did he last move outside his everyday routine? When did he last do something different? He decides that he does not want to dwell on such things; as the image fades for a second time, Arthur fears that he is simply collecting more and more things to worry about.

Without warning, the receptionist checks her PS, picks out a paper from the bottom of the smaller pile in front of her, and calls out a number. Her unpleasantly harsh voice breaks into the relative quietness in the room, causing Arthur to once again lose his train of thought. He thinks of all the people in front of him who are possibly also applying emergency brakes to their own thought patterns, which, like his, are most probably erratic and illogical. While the room is still reverberating from the unexpected sound, and thoughts are dangerously skidding to some kind of stop, the receptionist drops the piece of paper into a bin at the side of her desk, and after a short space of time the woman who is the owner of the number slowly rises to her feet, looking slightly dazed and not completely sure of the connection between the intrusive noise still echoing around the room and its reality - the reality of having to cross a threshold to something that is unknown. She moves towards the door, doubtlessly conscious of the many eyes following her every step. Arthur thinks of all the unanswered questions that must be floating invisibly in the air above her and around her; questions that will not be answered until she is on the other side of the door.

Or perhaps she knows exactly what is behind that door. The thought, coming as if from nowhere, pushes aside all of Arthur's other thoughts. Perhaps he is the only one in the room who does not know what is beyond the waiting room. He looks around quickly and thinks: are all these people simply looking forward to a routine health examination or dental check? Or perhaps they are here to discuss changes to paperwork with a lawyer?

He is aware that his imagination is running riot, but he has no reason to expect that others might be experiencing the room (and the reason they have been called to the room) any differently to himself. He watches the woman carefully, his stomach involuntarily doing a series of invisible somersaults. Is the woman stressed, worried, afraid? Sitting behind the woman, and unable to see her face properly, even as she walks across the room, he is not completely sure.

He tries to think of something else - anything at all - but his mind refuses to move away from the door. He has been in the waiting room for several hours, and although more than ten people have already gone through the door, none of them have returned, so it is obviously not a two-way door. He feels constricted by an unreasonable fear that is slowly seeping through him, filling every part of his body, and his mind rushes off on another tangent where it is overwhelmed by the image of a large, open furnace into which people are being prodded and shoved. Whether the image is dependent on a handful of mediaeval paintings depicting hell that Arthur, as a boy, had seen in an art book is totally irrelevant; all that is important is the image itself in the bizarre context of the room, the receptionist, and the letter. Arthur's imagination does not have to go into overdrive for him to be able to see the surly-looking furnace assistants regaled with horns and pitchforks.

Then, almost as quickly as the image first appeared, the flames and the furnace assistants, or devils, fade into a new image of a firing squad facing a blindfolded figure - Arthur wonders: is it himself? - about to be executed. But before the order to shoot is given, and while Arthur is still wondering if he is the target of the line of rifles, the image breaks up and disappears, and he is confronted by yet another image that spreads out and fills his mind.

The new image, an image of a gurney with straps and a pseudo-medical person standing nearby with a large needle filled with some kind of life-ending fluid, is no more reassuring than the previous images, and he tries to force a completely different image into play - a railway station with a smiling attendant handing out tickets to some far-away destination - but, of all the images, he knows that this one is the most unlikely.

Although he has always had his doubts and fears about the Change and Unitas, he tells himself that his imagination is taking too much control. At the same time he knows that there has to be something behind the door, and, if it is not a doctor's surgery, or something similar, then what is it? There may not be furnaces or firing squads, but Arthur has read about different forms of torture, and he is squeamish about having his fingernails forcibly removed or his limbs brutally pulled out of alignment with his body.

He tries unsuccessfully to recall the image of the railway station and the friendly attendant. Instead, his mind is once again pulled towards the word *static*. He has still not decided whether it is he who is static or whether it is his environment that is static or whether static is the wrong word altogether. It is possible that *lacking in change* might apply on one of the many levels that make up his own personal world, but he is quite certain that on the important all-comprising level that ties everything together, there has been an excessive and unwarranted amount of change.

Arthur's anxiety has always been a problem for him. A few years after the Change, and shortly after Rowena had walked out on him, his nervousness and unease reached unprecedented levels. He had just finished moving into a new flat in the orange concrete tower block when he walked down to the train station and tried to throw himself under a train. He probably would have succeeded, but he was thwarted by a guard and a civic-minded citizen who, seeing what was about to happen, grabbed hold of him and grappled him to the hard, cold platform as the train thundered past. In hospital, dazed, medicated, and, if possible, even more depressed, he tried to explain to the psychiatrist that he had been sitting in his kitchen, drinking tea, when, without any kind of psychic warning, he had been suddenly confronted by the very clear and unmistakable realization that the flat on the third floor of the orange building was all he could ever hope to expect from life; it was the ultimate peak, and there was nowhere else for him to go. Empty years, not yet lived, stretched out in front of him like a long, knotted rope, and he did not feel that he could cope with the fact that this was all there was and that there was nothing more. The psychiatrist was not especially sympathetic, possibly because he did not completely understand. He prescribed tablets and a course of face-to-face therapy, and he suggested that, instead of focusing on such negative thoughts, Arthur should look around himself and contemplate the greatness and the complexity of the society in which he now lived.

Arthur took the pills and attended the therapy sessions with a young, and very eager, counsellor. He could not see that the Change had resulted in anything positive, but he finally had to admit that positive and negative were extremely subjective concepts, and what one person claimed to be negative could well be positive from someone else's perspective. The counsellor felt that this was a great step forwards in Arthur's rehabilitation, and Arthur, having realized that he was probably not going to be able to explain to anyone what he *really* felt, nodded compliantly while inside his head he could still see the long knotted rope heading off into his future.

As much as he may have wanted, he could not change the political system; instead, he decided he would have to protect himself from it. He would build up his own psychological fortress by analysing things, not only in relation to themselves but also in relation to things adjacent to them and beyond them. He would continue to construct routines and rituals that would protect him while rendering him immune from all the negativity that had seeped into his world. As the years progressed, the myriad patterns began to run his life: if patterns collided or collapsed, his day was ruined before it had even started, and he would have to quickly invent ways of neutralising the situation and returning his life to something that resembled normal.

After his twelve-month brush with the Mental Health Department following his unsuccessful attempt to imitate Anna Karenina's tragic end, Arthur decided that he was the only person who really understood himself, and that he was the only person who could form his immediate environment into something that was both safe and liveable. Once all of this became clear to him, he concentrated on reinforcing his fortress and perfecting his routines.

While he is still worrying about static environments, the woman and the door, and what might, or might not, be beyond the room, part of his mind continues to think about waiting rooms in general. A long string of seemingly unconnected and, at the same time, connected thoughts twirls and then unravels, and he finds himself wondering whether waiting requires a physical room. He thinks: perhaps waiting is more about a *waiting space,* and the idea of a specific room is superfluous. Even *space* is the wrong word, he thinks, because where the waiting is done is of little or no importance: it is the actual *action* of waiting that is the important thing, the central, unavoidable thing.

Not knowing why he is in the waiting room or what is behind the door, he is uncomfortably thankful that he was not the one who had to leave his seat and exit the waiting room. A routine health check is beginning to look most attractive, and fifteen minutes in a dentist's chair is absolutely the preferred option to all the other pos- sibilities that have been milling around in his head. He tries to assure himself that there is nothing at all to worry about, even though he knows that he will eventually have to leave his seat and walk through that door. Once he has passed through the door, he is fully aware that the door will close behind him, leaving him to confront whatever it is that lurks behind it.

Rowena had always said that he was imagining things and that Unitas was neither better nor worse than any other government they had had. She accepted Arthur's point that the Party had implemented a whole lot of restrictions and unusual regulations, but had then added, waving her hands in all directions, that things were actually being done. She claimed that society as a whole felt safer, more contained, and that wealth was being distributed much more evenly The widening rift between the haves and the have-nots had shrunk; in fact, there was no rift any longer; everyone had suddenly found that they were standing together on the same piece of ground. She did admit that she no longer had the same number of freedoms that she had had before Unitas, but, like with anything, it was a case of give and take. Nothing could ever be completely perfect.

When Rowena talked like that, Arthur listened without being at all convinced. Many people thought the same as Rowena, but he knew that they were all wrong. Eventually, they would wake up and realize just how wrong they had been; there was no way of convincing them to think otherwise before they were ready to understand.

He tries to forget Rowena and what she thought and what she said, and instead he racks his brain, wondering when he had his last medical, when he last saw the dentist, and when he did his yearly tax review. His mind, however, will not focus steadily on just one thing, and his head fills up with images of drills, dentists, stethoscopes, disinterested lab assistants, badly sorted figures and, for some reason, a calendar on his PS with reminders scrawled against every date for that particular month. Reminders that he cannot read.

When he glances over the ten or so people remaining in the waiting room, he wonders if anyone else is feeling exactly the same as he is: sorry for the woman who had been called, but silently relieved that - at least this time - it was someone else and not them. On the other hand, if they are fully aware of what is behind the door then they are probably not sorry for anyone, and they most likely have no reason to feel relieved.

It is the *not knowing* that is eating into him, corrupting his sanity, twisting around his mind and filling it with Goya-like images.

The silence reaches a crescendo and then fades into an eerie stillness as the woman finally disappears from view. As the door in the front wall closes, Arthur feels how the atmosphere in the room abruptly reverts to normal: it is almost as though the person never existed, never sat on one of the aqua chairs, was never called to the door, never passed through the door. All that can be heard is the sound of the receptionist's knitting needles, the sound of the clock, the bright sound of chairs occasionally moving on the hard floor. The unformed questions that had filled the space only moments before sullenly retreat to the corners of the room, ready to spring out again when the next number is called.

Arthur has never really adjusted to the idea of numbers; he can still remember a time when everyone had names instead of numbers. He only ever thinks of himself as *Arthur*, but since the Change people are always referred to by their numbers, and people from before the Change have also been issued with numbers. Everyone has been ordered to forget his or her name: names foster concepts of individuality and originality, and Unitas is all about the whole not the individual. Unitas has made it very clear that society and the interests of the whole should always be placed before the interests, and the imagined needs, of the individual.

Arthur wonders whether anyone can be ordered to forget something. He has always felt that the fact that one must remember what it is that one must forget makes the exercise completely impossible. But many people from his generation - the generation before the Change - now swear that they have completely forgotten their names. Arthur tends to regard such assurances with much scepticism, at the same time as he understands the drive to survive in a society where the individual is no longer of any real importance.

In spite of his need to survive, Arthur has never had any intention of forgetting his name. He clings to it as one of the very few things that he has left that identifies him as the person he really is. Nowadays people normally just point to their badge or to the number stitched on their shirt when they introduce themselves: the custom of using names in conversation dropped out of use a long while ago. There is something special in the sound of a name passing between the lips, a sound that can never be replicated by listing off a string of digits.

He suddenly remembers a nightmare he had a few nights back. He must have been hiking or rock climbing, and while negotiating the side of a cliff he looked up at the sky, which was beginning to cloud over, and in that split second he lost concentration and slid at least fifty metres down the smooth steep rock.

He tries to remember if he thought anything as he fell, but it was a dream, and it is thankfully already beginning to fade at the edges. Trying to reconstruct the situation mentally, he concludes that if he thought of anything as he fell, it was probably an awareness that whatever it was it would have been the very last thing he would ever think. He can remember clearly that there were no bushes to catch, or even slow down, his fall, and beneath him was the black and pounding ocean.

As he tries to recall the dream, he remembers the sense of horror, and how he attempted to intervene in the dream and somehow lift himself back on to the cliff. It did not work, and he remained lying on the narrow finger of pebbly beach. While he was mentally trying to change the course of the dream, he noted how the tide was on its way in. The water was already washing around his feet - he could sense it, but because it was a dream he could not feel it. When he looked upwards, hoping for a way out, all he could see was the smooth, black granite walls of the cliff.

Arthur inhales very deeply and then exhales slowly. He does this several times before adjusting his sitting position by leaning forwards and then back. He rolls his shoulders, first forwards and then backwards, and turns his head a few times from side to side. The clock on the wall behind him shows that it is already a quarter past five, which means that he has been in the waiting room for more than three hours. From his place on the right hand side of the second row of chairs, he wearily regards the backs of the people sitting in front of him. The dozen or so people who have already been called to the door at the front of the room were all in the waiting room before he arrived. Given that most of them have been replaced by new people, he wonders just how much longer he will have to wait. Whether or not he can consider himself lucky so far is debatable - it all depends on what is on the other side of that door - but if it is luck that has kept him on his seat in the waiting room then it is luck with a very restricted use-by date.

While he is thinking about the number of people who

have been called to the door and whether it might be his turn next, a thought that has been pressing against the back of his mind all afternoon pushes to the forefront and demands his full attention.

Perhaps it all has nothing to do with luck, or good fortune, or karma, or even despotic governments; things that, in reality, are so tenuous and indefinite. It may well be that there is a reasonable explanation for his having been called to floor thirty-six, but if this is not the case and the reason is more sinister, then he has already reached the end of the line allotted to him, and, no matter how he feels about it, there is obviously nowhere else for him to go. He has undoubtedly passed the point where things could have gone in one of two directions - now there is only one direction and it is not the direction Arthur himself would have chosen.

Perhaps all the people in the room have reached the end of their allotted line, he thinks as he looks out over the heads of the people in front of him, reflecting on the fact that some lines are obviously longer than others.

His thinking is on a roll. Although it is an outlandish idea, Arthur wonders if, on entering the waiting room, he somehow moved from being alive to being dead. Perhaps he has already gone past the end of his line without fully realizing. He toys with the idea for a few seconds, thinking that it might explain the absurdity of his situation, but then he irritably discards the idea, doubting that it is possible to pass from life to death and still be aware that a change has taken place. As far as he is concerned, death means an end to everything: perception, thought, imagination, analysis. He feels that it must be like a blackness that absorbs and envelops, the same blackness that he imagines is all that exists billions and billions of kilometres beyond the point where he is standing, or sitting. But not knowing much about cosmology or astronomy, he wonders if there is such a place and decides that a better analogy would be a black hole. Not that he knows any more about black holes, but he has heard that they do not reflect light, and from what he can gather they must be more contained than an area of space well beyond the constraints of his numerical imagination.

His thinking brakes suddenly, and he decides that he likes the image of 'life lines' dissipating into a black hole. He completely stops his train of thought while he considers death as a vast, black hole, realizing that it makes no difference how he decides to define it: no one living has any way of knowing, and the dead... He shrugs, thinking that it is impossible to know what the dead think, or do not think, or even if they actually think. He decides that everything - outer space, black holes, and explanations pertaining to life and death - is simply a matter of conjecture.

However, although similarities between the ideas of entering a waiting room and slipping seamlessly from life to death somewhat appeal to him, in a morbid kind of way, he quickly discards the thought that he may have already passed into this second state. He is aware that he is extremely stressed and overly anxious, and his thoughts are rushing away from him in too many different directions. He concentrates on pulling them back to some form of normal thinking. If he truly believed that he were dead, then he would not be worrying about anything any more. He would be beyond worrying; he would be beyond the confines of the waiting room, beyond the discomfort of plastic aqua-coloured chairs and certainly beyond the control of the very rude receptionist sitting behind him at the far side of the room. But he *is* worrying and that, if anything, tells him that he is still very much alive.

Nevertheless the thought of death, whether it is correct in his case or not, sends a long ribbon of cold rippling down through his body. He surveys the annoyingly bright room and wonders if passing from life to death is simply the process of being absorbed or reabsorbed into the sun or the light or another kind of life force. He vaguely remembers having heard somewhere that without the sun there would be no life.

He shudders involuntarily and becomes aware that, in spite of the warm room, he is shivering. He mentally focuses on stopping both the shuddering and the shivering, but his body and his mind seem to be moving along very different tracks. Although he really wants to forget everything that has anything to do with death equating with a black hole or a place in outer space, his thoughts keep creeping back to his previous thoughts. While he tries to think of other things, his mind is focused on death, the importance of light, and the possibility of death being some kind of osmosis or permeation involving the sun, and then, in an effort to take control, he returns to his earlier thought that if he were dead he would most definitely not be worrying about such things.

He presses his fingernails into the palms of his hands, feeling a sudden sharp pain that confirms that he is undeniably still alive. He draws a deep breath and moves a little on the hard plastic chair. The fact that he is still alive and can reason and think somewhat logically, if erratically, boosts his confidence even if his future looks especially bleak.

He takes a quick glance around the room, and wonders if other people's thoughts are operating along similar lines, or whether everyone is completely confident that there is nothing ominous waiting for them on the other side of the door. By leaning forwards, Arthur is able to see most of the people in the back row of chairs, and, apart from a couple at the far end of the row chatting quietly, those he can see either look extremely bored or have closed their eyes. Are they sleeping, confident that nothing disastrous is about to happen to them, or have they retreated into themselves, locking out images and sounds that might cause them undue distress? Arthur has no way of knowing, but, having finally gained some control over his thoughts, he forces them to move in a different direction, and he recalls images of his orange concrete building, his job at the Department of Discarded and Lost Property, and then, finally, his childhood.

Apart from occasional visits to the dentist and all the normal angst associated with school and growing up, he believes that his childhood was mostly happy: he cannot remember that it was particularly unhappy, nor is he overwhelmed by memories and images of himself being miserable and downhearted. By the time he started school, three of his grandparents were still living - one of them in the same town, the other two far enough away to warrant day-long excursions and sometimes even week-end stays. He also had a number of aunts and uncles and a handful of cousins, both younger and older than himself - in other words, he belonged to an average family.

He lived with his parents and a younger brother in a small red-brick house in what would have been termed a pleasant street where there were many other similar small red-brick houses. Each house had a neat front garden, most of them complete with one or two evergreen trees or bushes, and between the houses and the road a narrow strip of grass bordered the footpath. In the summer the grass near the footpath, like the grass in the front gardens, turned yellow-brown and, almost overnight, would become home to patches of bindi-eyes - small, sharp burs that pierced his unprotected bare feet, suggesting to him that not everything in life could be trusted and that, if possible, one should always be prepared.

Arthur's brother, unlike Arthur, was noticeably extroverted. He was also intellectually and physically gifted; while Arthur crammed and agonized, his brother sailed through school and, later, university, at the same time as he captained the cricket team and won accolades for his swimming and tennis.

Their father was an engineer with the word civil attached, and their mother worked in an office. As a child, Arthur was never quite sure what his parents did: his father commuted to the city and was sometimes away for several days at a time, while every day, Monday to Friday, his mother took the red bus from the bus stop at the end of the street to an office in another town.

By the time he knew more about civil engineering, the Change was well under way, and he had already lost contact with both his father and his mother. Perhaps his father could have told him about the bridges and roads he had designed and built, though there was also a chance that his father was simply one of the many small cogs in the bridge-building, road-construction wheel, and that the whole both negated and obliterated the many parts.

During the years preceding the Change, a further two grandparents had died and his father's mother, now well into her eighties, had been moved to a home at a considerable distance from where Arthur lived.

Technically orphaned after his parents disappeared, Arthur did consider turning to his aunts and uncles, or even his cousins, for both support and advice, but his relatives, like small pieces of shredded paper on a windy day, had all vanished. After several months he finally managed to connect with an older cousin, but the cousin, like Arthur, was disorientated and depressed, and after promising to keep in touch they both drifted off in different directions.

Arthur reflects on the fact that he is thinking of all his family in the past: he wonders whether any of them are still alive and, if so, where they are; apart from his cousin, he has not seen any of them for almost twenty years. Even if his parents and other relatives are now deceased - which is possible, though, apart from his grandmother, probably unlikely - the majority of his cousins as well as his brother must still be alive. He is quite sure that wherever his brother is he is most probably coping particularly well: Arthur could not imagine his brother being told to present himself at floor thirty-six on a particular day of a particular month, and if such a thing were to happen he cannot imagine that his brother would be especially perturbed; he would have known exactly what to do. While Arthur worries incessantly about most things, his brother accepted everything as a matter of course and did not seem to worry about anything. Arthur would like to have know where he was, though; apart from their obvious social and emotional differences, they probably had more in common than they realized.

He finds it disconcerting that his thoughts are seeking out his childhood, his 'before'. Normally he tries to keep this early part of his life completely cut off from the 'now': there is no point in thinking about what has been and what can no longer be retrieved. Although he tries to push his thoughts in other directions, images of his mother - fair and plump - and his father - tall, thin and wearing glasses - insist on flickering across his mind. More images, these ones including his brother, George - tall, fair, and not wearing glasses - and even himself tumble one over the other, until Arthur feels, for a moment at least, that he is back in that other time, the time he tries not to think about. Things could have been so different; he feels inexplicably sorry for his family and so hopelessly sorry for himself.

Arthur's thoughts veer sharply away from the pictures of family life on the outskirts of the town and brake in front of the word *Unitas*. For him it is not a word as such but a realization, an understanding, an awareness, a blackness, a fear.

For Arthur Unitas was both the end and the beginning. It was because of Unitas that everything changed.

Arthur makes a concerted effort to move his thoughts away from Unitas and back to how life was before. Before everything changed. He sighs and shifts once again on the hard chair. He finds it impossible not to think of Unitas, especially given the fact that if Unitas had never existed, there was a pretty good chance, as far as he could see it, that he would not be sitting on such a chair in such a room.

In the brightly lit room his unrestrained thoughts return without warning to the question of being alive or being dead, the irrational situation into which he has been thrown, and, finally, whether the situation is irrational or whether it could simply be his imagination running away with him. Although logic is trying to bring some order to his imagination, and although he knows without a doubt that he is still alive, he begins to entertain the idea that he *actually* may have died a long while ago.

The ideas that propelled Unitas to power began decades before Arthur was born, and now, so many years later, there was no real consensus of opinion as to how, or why, Unitas came into being. Arthur had heard that back in that time when the ideas that would eventually give birth to Unitas were still unformed and consequently unspoken, the world was trembling on the edge of annihilation. Countries were at war with each other while environmental catastrophes were replacing each other quicker than the media were able to report on them. Waves of refugees were moving, first in one direction, and then, when unrest broke out in places previously deemed safe, in another, completely different, direction. As politics slid from the left and centre towards the far right, power blocs were rapidly changing, and those who felt power slipping from their grasp were trying to do all they could to halt the inevitable. The very structure of society was breaking up as people focused entirely on themselves and everything that they felt was essential to their own, personal happiness. But no one really knew what happiness was any longer - the concept had become caught up with the need to possess - and the people manufacturing the things that people wanted to own became more powerful than the political structures that were there to restrain them. In the end, everything was sucked into something that resembled a huge hamster wheel that turned faster and faster, spinning out waste and discarded dreams as the world became hotter and drier and everything descended into chaos.

No one disputed that the world of several decades past had been on the verge of collapse, and it was recognized that most countries, pushed by greed and ignorance to very edge of an imminent fall, blanched and, at the very last moment, took a few frantic steps backwards. Most countries grabbed hold of whatever was at hand to stop themselves from falling. In the country where Arthur would eventually see the light of day the thing people grabbed hold of was Unitas.

Many people later argued that the chaotic situation was in itself sufficient to give birth to Unitas; others, although they conceded that a world descending into turmoil could easily throw up a movement like Unitas, felt that there were other, more significant, reasons why Unitas appeared and why it eventually remained.

One theory was that the basic idea had been imported into the country years before the whole world went into meltdown and that it had remained under cover, quietly germinating, until the time was right for it to sprout.

Another was that it was the brainchild of a small group made up of business people and a number of politicians from opposing political parties, all of whom had been frustrated by political systems where the many worth-while motions and ideas put forward in parliament were quashed, simply because the game of opposition had become bigger and more important than any idea of service to the community. As they saw it, time that could have been used to create and realize a vision for both the present and the future was being wasted on useless and egotistical squabbling.

Others believed that Unitas was simply an integral part of the power play of one of those two or three power blocs that had been vying with each other to eventually control the entire world.

Whatever it was that launched the ideas so central to Unitas, Arthur knew that in the past it was considered normal for political parties and governments to come and go. He also knew that some stayed longer than they should have, while others that may have had the vision and the will to change things for the better often disappeared before anyone was fully aware of their existence. Unitas, which was finally swept into power when Arthur was still in his teens, had no intention of disappearing: it had come to stay.

It was the party that, in the months leading up to the general election, had promised the people all the things they so desperately wanted, but, once elected, had tweaked meanings, removed both core and non-core promises and had added lots of small print. Over time, opposition was gradually stifled and eventually abolished. Unitas was a party with one objective: a unified, controlled society.

The country that had always considered itself a democracy had silently morphed into a dictatorship. At first this change had been gradual, subtle, and unobtrusive, and then, when everything was more or less in place, things changed pace, and the final phase of the transformation was both sudden and brutal. People looked at each other in amazement and disbelief, wondering how such a thing could have been allowed to happen. Could they have done anything to have stopped it happening? Could it possibly have been their fault, or would it have happened no matter what they had done or had not done? Others wondered if it may have been a good thing - at least the bickering between the Parties had stopped and it felt as though someone was finally in control.

Nevertheless, concepts concerning basic beliefs - political, religious, and otherwise - had been thoroughly revised, with Unitas now playing the part of God. There was nothing else but Unitas: free will was taboo; personal freedom was a vague memory from the past. New rules and regulations were drawn up, creating impenetrable, unscalable barriers, while the people locked inside were subjected to a barrage of enforced disciplines they had either never before encountered or never taken seriously. People soon realized that there was very little they could do: objection was out of the question; as Arthur understood it, dissenters were people who simply disappeared.

Arthur tries to pick up sounds beyond the waiting room. For a moment he imagines that he can hear the far-off sound of a dentist's drill. In any other situation, he would have found the sound more than slightly stressful, but now he finds that he is clinging to it as the only sign that the waiting room is a normal waiting room and that whatever is behind the door is also normal.

The sound he thinks he can hear is very faint, and although he is straining his ears he cannot be perfectly sure that he is really hearing anything at all. He could easily be imagining the sound, but, if it truly exists, it would redefine his present situation as something less terrifying and slightly more benign.

He rubs his ears a couple of times and glances at the people in his row of chairs. He would really like to know if any of them have heard sounds coming from beyond the room. He considers asking the man sitting next to him, but he is not really sure what to say. He does not want to come across as a complete idiot. Perhaps he could simply ask why the man is in the waiting room, but on second thoughts Arthur feels that the question is too personal. If the man needs to see the doctor about a sexually transmitted disease or if he has evaded tax for the past three years, it is unlikely that he will want to talk about it to a perfect stranger. Instead, Arthur smiles hurriedly at him and then focuses his gaze on the front wall.

The occasional scraping of chairs on the floor, the sudden, unexpected coughs, the hushed sounds of quiet conversations, and all the other disparate noises that fill rooms like waiting rooms form an auditory screen between Arthur and whatever might be behind the door. He can no longer hear what he thought could have been a drill, and he is now certain that he only imagined it, in the same way that he may be imagining footsteps, muffled voices, and even uncoordinated strands of music from beyond the wall.

Arthur decides that what he really needs is coffee - black and very strong. He runs his eyes around the room, almost as though expecting to see a coffee cart standing against one of the walls. Although he is aware that coffee is not part of the furnishings, his mind, now focused on the dark, aromatic beverage, will not let go of the image. He can almost taste and smell the sharp, yet rounded, bitterness of the hot liquid as it moves around his mouth and down his throat. Even in his imagination the lingering warm taste soothes him and removes him to a more pleasant place.

Beyond any doubt he needs coffee.

Thinking of coffee makes him aware that he would also like to visit the toilet, and he surveys the room, his thoughts weaving around both coffee carts and toilets.

He is quite sure that he has not given any thought, up until this moment, to either toilets or refreshments, his mind having been completely occupied with why he might be where he is and what might be behind the door, but now he is unable to think of anything else. Although he does not imagine that a coffee cart will suddenly appear at the front of the room, he feels that any waiting room worth the name should have access to a toilet.

His eyes scan the walls of the waiting room, looking for a door that he may have missed. He feels that he knows the room with its white walls and timber flooring inside out, and as far as he can tell there are only two doors - the door by which he entered and the door at the front of the room by which he will eventually leave.

He tries to remember if he has seen anyone else looking for a toilet, but it is not something that has stuck in his memory. He considers asking the person sitting next to him, but then wonders if the question could be out of place. He has already turned his head in the man's direction, and the question is on his lips, but he decides not to say anything, sighs, and slowly rises to his feet.

As he does so he can feel that the receptionist's eyes are fixated on him, and he expects to hear her strident voice splitting the relative silence of the room. Sitting at the very end of the back row, Arthur does not have to disturb anyone, and once he is on his feet he walks past the back row of chairs to the receptionist's desk. He is annoyed with himself that such an insignificant request should be causing his heart to beat faster and his mouth to feel numb and dry. He holds his right hand behind his back and continually taps each of his fingers on his thumb: if she answers him when his ring finger is on his thumb then he will get a positive answer.

The question is simple enough: he has asked it many times previously in a variety of places and situations without feeling as though the question will condemn him to execution. The woman reluctantly removes her eyes from her PS and looks at him as though he might be an insect she is about to squash.

Arthur's heart is beating even faster; he wonders if perhaps he might have a heart attack, which, if the truth be told, could be positive as it would eliminate most, if not all, of his present problems. He taps his ring finger with his thumb ten times, hoping that it will help move everything in a positive direction.

Keeping one hand on her PS, she explains to Arthur that the toilets are in the corridor, to the left of the waiting room, and with her free hand she pushes a small button on her desk. Arthur can hear a slight sound as the locking device for the entry door releases.

Arthur nods his thanks, and with his thumb still firmly pressing against his ring finger, he walks to the door and opens it. As he exits the room he looks back at the receptionist, but she no longer seems aware of him; all her attention is obviously focused on her screen.

As the door closes behind him, Arthur experiences something akin to a small rush of exhilaration, almost as though he has been set free - a feeling only emphasized by the sudden, somewhat frightening, realization that the door only opens inwards from the corridor and is locked from the waiting room side. He wonders briefly if he should continue down the corridor and take the lift to the ground floor but realizes that such a course of action would most probably be extremely foolhardy.

Even as he is being swamped by competing feelings of both liberation and anxiety, he is fully aware of the absurdity of the situation, if, as he is hoping, he is simply waiting for a routine medical check up. With the waiting room behind him, he turns to the left and begins to walk back along the corridor in the direction of the lift.

He cannot stop thinking about the fact that although the door to the waiting room opens easily from the corridor, it is locked from the opposite direction. This obviously means that people are not supposed to return to the corridor from the waiting room. He wonders why, but he does not want his imagination taking charge again, so he discards the thought and concentrates on the fact that he has finally found a sliver of normality on to which he can hold: a waiting room with a toilet - all perfectly normal and totally within one's expectations. He thinks: perhaps he should have also asked the receptionist about coffee.

The doors to the toilets - one for males and one for females - are almost unnoticeable, being painted the same colour as the walls. Arthur is not amazed that he missed them when he was in the corridor earlier: he was far too focused on what was at the end of the corridor, and he was certainly not on the lookout for a toilet. Now, when he looks closer at the doors, he can see that they are completely flush with the wall and that the only thing denoting their purpose are the small black stylized figures.

Arthur opens the door to the male toilet, which is somewhat cramped, sterile and minus any form of window. He stands for a moment, his back against the door, revelling in the fact that he is completely on his own - no difficult receptionist and no one else anywhere around. Cocooned between the sterile white tiles he can almost pretend that there is no waiting room and no door through which he must eventually pass.

To what?

He breathes in and out deeply several times. The isolation and the quietness afforded by the room is calming him. He counts the tiles on the opposite wall, first vertically and then horizontally. The washbasin breaks up the tiles at waist level, and disrupts his counting. He begins again, higher up. The counting and the numbers are helping him: he feels more in control.

But, apart from flushing himself down the toilet, which, even had it been possible, is not particularly pleasant to contemplate, Arthur realizes that he cannot use the toilet as a way of escaping his present situation. Not that he had expected to see a door with a sign: *Exit here for the normal world*, but in his present stressed state nothing would really surprise him.

Life had been reasonably normal (although, *normal*, Arthur argued with himself, could never be anything more than relative. Relative to what? he wondered) until he was nineteen. Unitas had already been in power for about five years, but then, shortly after his nineteenth birthday, the world as he had known it suddenly fell away from him. Looking back, he felt that it was as though Earth had tipped on its pivotal axis or perhaps even begun rotating in the opposite direction. Within what seemed like a very short time the entire country was divided into a patchwork of sectors, each sector being a complete independent unit, sometimes consisting of several small towns, occasionally cutting across existing town borders. In the years since Unitas had first established itself as the governing entity, the village atmosphere of his town - now known only as Sector 24781 - had been more or less obliterated, as tall orange, grey, yellow and white blocks of high-rise flats were erected alongside the simple family homes of a long-gone era. The move towards such communal living had begun in the cities decades before Unitas, with high-rise tower blocks being built on the rubble of small, single-storey dwellings, but, after the Change, Arthur had seen how the trend had accelerated, and how it had also quickly spread to the smaller towns. Had it been at all possible, he was quite sure that the new government would have razed all existing homes and packed everyone into tower blocks. Apart from such a project being an indefensible waste of materials and manpower, the estimated logistics and cost of putting such an outlandish idea into practice would have been so staggering that no one in their right mind would have even considered it, something for which Arthur was thankful. Instead, it was decided that in the future no new single-dwelling homes would be built and that, eventually, most people would live in tower blocks. In the meantime, Administration bulldozed some homes on the outskirts of Sector 24781, turning the areas into parkland. Beyond the innocent-looking parkland they built intrusion detection systems based on infra-red array sensors. The invisible fences not only kept intruders out, they also stopped people from leaving the sector without permission.

At the centre of each sector, or as close to the centre as possible, a number of multi-storey government buildings formed a close-knit hub, looking out over the rest of the sector. In the early years, while Unitas was possibly fearing some kind of insurrection, families were deliberately scattered between different sectors. No one was given any information as to where family members had been sent, and somewhere along the way Arthur lost contact with his parents and George. He contacted the authorities on many occasions, but no one could, or would, give him any answers. Finally he understood that his constant questioning was labelling him a trouble-maker, and that his best option was to remain quiet and to passively melt into the background with everyone else; his questions were never going to be answered: he was never going to find out what had happened to his family.

Arthur's home was one of those that was turned into

parkland; while he was still protesting the unfairness of it all, he was allocated a small unit in an orange concrete building next to other identical orange and grey buildings, all of them patterned with shiny glass windows and stainless-steel balconies. He was on his own, and he now had a number instead of a name. His life had been turned upside down, but for all it was worth he was still alive.

The shift that preceded, and indeed caused, the precarious tilt to the Earth's rotation did not happen overnight: alterations to the judicial and legal systems, and the transformation of social systems, both physically and theoretically, had begun the moment Unitas ascended to power, and they were carried out so efficiently and so gradually that no one was really aware of anything out of the ordinary until that moment when the Earth tilted, and everyone realized that there was absolutely nothing they could do about it.

Whether the idea behind Unitas - to create a unified and motivated government - had evolved from that group of politicians and business people, or whether it had sprung from some other source, the idea was initially considered by a small majority to be sound and even commendable. The obvious fact that Unitas would have to be able to operate without opposition in order to achieve its goal did not seem to deter these people, though a number of people who had been introduced to the idea, and who were still capable of thinking for themselves, did not take long to put an equals sign between 'operating without opposition' and totalitarianism.

In spite of such warning signals, the popularity of Unitas grew. In the beginning, all those decades ago, information about the party spread in a fairly erratic and somewhat clandestine fashion; however, as the years passed and the movement became more established, the party's policies came out into the open. Many people were attracted by the idea of a political party that, unhampered, might be able to get things done; others were fearful of something that seemed like a grab for absolute power, and they feared where this power might inevitably lead. There were few people still alive who could remember the dictatorships of the twentieth century, but memories and warnings had been handed down through the generations, and some people felt that they were warnings worth heeding.

Faithful followers of Unitas, well versed in the party's policies, began to infiltrate factories, schools and universities, hospitals, churches, entertainment centres, and shopping malls. And the media. By the time the democratically-held election propelled Unitas into power, most people were able to spout all the right slogans, and they were certain that Unitas was the only way of righting a failed system: finally things would start happening.

To a point they were right, but things did not start happening exactly in the way they had imagined.

Arthur does wonder at times just what it means: being alive. He may look on himself as a living being - though every so often he does have his doubts - but he is no longer certain that he is still the person he was before the Change. There have been numerous times when he has thought that it would have been much better had he been demolished along with his home on the outskirts of the town.

In his late teens, as the world around him was beginning to spin out of orbit, he set about reading as many of the dystopian novels as he could get hold of. He found *Brave New World* in the small, brown bookcase in the lounge room - indeed it was *Brave New World* that set him on the dystopian path - but he did not have any of the other books, so he borrowed some of them from the local library and others from a friend whose father was a teacher and had a bookcase that covered one whole wall of his large study. For Arthur that bookcase symbolized everything that lay beyond what he would have called ordinary. He may have been reliant on his routines and the security of knowing what was happening around him, but at the same time there was something inside of him that was drawn to the unconventional and the unknown.

While he clung to the familiar his imagination created a world that was different, exciting and yet safe. The bookcase embodied both the excitement and the safety; it was the most wonderful thing he had ever seen.

Fanatical about most things, he took somewhat fragmented, and often incoherent, notes on each book, excited by ideas that he perceived as being similar and by others that he felt were completely unique. He had been intrigued by the images that Huxley and Zamyatin painted, and disturbed by Koestler's description of a police state. But, after several weeks of intensive reading and study, he decided that these grim, depressing books were simply the figments of a few people's overly active imaginations. He decided that he did not belong to the group of people who viewed them as being prophetic: they were entertaining in a morbid, frightening kind of way, but he felt that they were basically fanciful and unrelated to reality. As far as Arthur was concerned, modern-day society was constructed in such a way that no matter what happened it would ultimately protect itself from all such irrational and quite terrifying ideas. Although others hastened to remind him of past societies that had bordered on the dystopian, he found it unbelievable that anyone would want to mentally create such a society. Taking *Nineteen Eighty-Four* as an example, he insisted that all fictional dystopian societies were both irrational and completely avoidable. He felt sorry for Winston Smith, but he found it difficult to believe that anything like Big Brother and the Ministry of Love could literally exist. In real life, a government like that of Oceania would be overthrown long before it could impact the freedoms and the ideals of its citizens.

After the Change had established itself, he thought back to what he had read and to what he had thought and to what he had said, and he admitted to himself that he had been wrong.

He carefully stretches his legs and then pulls them back under his chair and wonders about the opposite to dystopian. Had there ever been anything that could be called a utopian society? At the moment, as far as Arthur is concerned, anything that is not Unitas has to be utopian, but if there has actually existed a utopian society completely on its own merits is something he cannot answer. Although democracies have all attempted to offer a semblance of equality and a certain amount of personal freedom, they could hardly be called utopian.

He wonders what he actually means by *utopian*.

Sitting on his chair, Arthur focuses his thoughts once more on all the things that might, or might not, be waiting for him on the other side of the door. Perhaps there is nothing more terrifying than a dentist or a taxation officer, but during all the time he has been sitting in the waiting room he has not seen anyone returning through the door. This is not a new observation - it has been clinging to his consciousness since he entered the waiting room - but it is an observation that is beginning to exacerbate his anxiety even further. Normally people leave and re-enter a waiting room through the same door. Then, unexpectedly, it occurs to him that the exit door from whatever is beyond the waiting room could be different and that it may not open out on to the waiting room. Perhaps there is a kind of exiting room instead. The thought helps him relax a little, and he feels his anxiety lessen as some of the tension breaks away from his neck and shoulders. He is annoyed that he may have been worrying about something that is quite obvious; yet, at the same time, he knows that he has cause to be worried: people who comment negatively on the system, however ambig-uously, simply disappear. Many people have already disappeared; no one knows what happens to them - it is as though they never existed.

In the early years of the new government, people began disappearing without warning. No one could say exactly how the disappearances took place - whether the people disappeared of their own accord or whether there was something more sinister at play. Arthur had anxiously discussed the disappearances with others, many of whom felt that he was reading something alarming into something that, in all probability, was quite normal. People often moved around, they argued, sometimes because of a new job, a new relationship or simply because of a need to see and experience different things. Not everyone was content to stay in the same place for ever.

But Arthur had heard it rumoured that any form of resistance to the system could trigger a disappearance, and he calculated that it was this fear of unknown retribution that kept the society from disintegrating; there was no point in objecting: it was easier and safer to keep one's head down, to remain in the shadows and to obey the rules. People who felt the same as Arthur were not happy, but they were alive, and as long as they were alive there was always a chance that things might eventually right themselves. Secretly these people looked forward to the day when things would change back to what they had been, even though they knew that the probability of that happening was more or less impossible.

Although Arthur did not voice his disagreement loudly like so many others, he did write letters in an effort to find his family. Perhaps his letter writing was sufficient for him to be called to Building C? He is not sure; it is years since he wrote those letters. There must be some other reason for his being called up now. Unless, of course, he is simply worrying about nothing, and there is a perfectly logical and innocent reason for him being where he is.

Arthur has always been a worrier. As a child, he not only worried about the dentist, but also about his school work, his parents dying and leaving him an orphan, whether he should wear his blue T-shirt or his pale grey polo, or whether the man standing next to his mother at the bus stop was a murderer. He also worried about the way his shoes stood next to each other under his bed, the pattern made by his food when it was dished up on his plate, the number of steps it took him to get from the front gate to the front door, how long he could hold his breath until the neighbour's dog barked, or the doorbell rang, or something else happened over which he himself had no control.

As he became older he continued to worry, but by then his worrying had taken on a slightly different slant, and it was usually not obvious to anyone but himself. He still counted steps and agonized over which packet of cornflakes he should take from the supermarket shelf, but he tried to keep his anxiety hidden. When people looked at him curiously, as though they wanted to ask something but did not know how to phrase the question, then Arthur knew that his anxiety was showing, and he would smile or sigh and, grabbing the closest cornflakes packet or putting a sudden stop to the stream of numbers - was it two hundred and eighty-five steps or was it two hundred and eighty-six? - would leave the shop or the workplace or the community hall, trying to look completely normal but knowing, somewhere inside of himself, that he was not completely normal and that his day had been thoroughly ruined.

Over the years, he has learnt to live within the limits of his anxiety; he has chosen to look on his compulsive, often obsessive, behaviour as part of himself, like hair or eye colour, and he has tried not to let it define him. As far as Arthur is concerned, everyone has anxiety problems to some degree; it is just a matter of accepting them and getting on with life. Long ago, he reached the conclusion that the main thing is being able to keep the anxiety at a level where it can be managed; however, just now in the waiting room he is rapidly approaching a point where his tension and worry are likely to get the upper hand.

At half past five, a young man sitting in the front row is called to the door. Arthur interrupts the erratic train of his thoughts to inhale deeply and feel comforted that once again it has been someone else's number and not his. At least, not this time. But he is not sure whether it makes sense to be happy about the reprieve or whether it may have been easier to have everything all over and done with. It is the waiting that is rapidly propelling him towards a state of madness. His head is aching and he can feel the tension returning to the back of his neck - a tension that runs all the way down through his body to his stomach, which is a tight, heavy lump somewhere in the centre of his body.

Arthur wonders about all the people who have already been called to the door: what happens to them on the other side of the door? Is there a dentist's surgery or a doctor's consulting room waiting for them? Or are they whisked away by a taxation officer wanting complimentary information regarding declared income tax? Or is the answer much more disturbing, even macabre?

Thinking about what might be ahead of him, Arthur wonders if it could be possible to simply walk out of the waiting room and return home. He could always say that he had changed his mind, or that he had suddenly remembered another appointment, or that he had promised his neighbour he would walk his dog. His head fills with an array of possible excuses, but when he thinks of the receptionist, sitting behind him, he is almost certain that none of them will be accepted.

What was it the letter said? *'Present yourself at reception on the thirty-sixth floor. Bring nothing with you.'* Arthur shakes his head. That was not a letter written by someone who would be happy to see him leave the waiting room before he has even been processed. His mind sidles around the word *processed*; the connotations are not pleasant. He thinks of processed foods, lines of immigrants, and a host of official procedures, and he wonders how he is to be processed. If, of course, that is what is about to happen. Yet again he forces his mind back to the letter. The word *process* did not appear on the sheet of grey paper; perhaps he has got it all wrong? Perhaps there is nothing ominous about the letter and nothing for him to be worried about?

He tries unsuccessfully to convince himself that he has nothing to worry about. He wonders if it might be worth trying out one of his many excuses on the receptionist. He turns in his chair and looks at her quickly before deciding that the idea is most probably dead before he has even had time to properly think it through.

If he cannot politely ask to be excused, he wonders if he could just leave - just stand up and walk out the door without saying anything to anyone. Then he remembers that the door is locked from the inside, and it is most unlikely that the receptionist is simply going to open it for him.

While Arthur is wishing that the door was like most other doors, opening freely in both directions, and that he were then brave enough to leave his place and walk out of the room, his thoughts meander around the idea of escape. He is fully aware that the idea is impossible, and the room offers no encouragement to continue thinking along such a line - there are only two doors and no windows - but he is unable to stop his thoughts from circling around the possibility. He suppresses a wry smile as he pictures himself climbing out of a window that does not exist on the thirty-sixth floor. He forces his thoughts back to the corridor leading to the waiting room and remembers that, apart from the doors to the toilets, he saw no other doors and absolutely nothing indicating an emergency exit stairwell. The part of his brain intent on escape reasons that if there were a stairwell, and if the door to the waiting room opened like a normal door, it could be worthwhile making a run for it, but the normal part of his brain is already analysing the idea and finding it extremely foolhardy.

Arthur pulls himself up short; he knows that it is not a possibility: he came in through one door and, whether he likes it or not, he will be going out via the second door. But the idea of an imaginary stairwell gives his thoughts free rein, and it removes his thoughts from the absurd reality of his situation.

In his imagination he is back in the corridor. Something tells him that there would be no point in returning to the lift at the far end of the corridor, as it is most likely programmed only to deliver people to the thirty-sixth floor, and any attempt to use it to return to the ground floor would probably set off a series of alarms. However, as luck would have it, there is an emergency exit stairwell opposite the waiting room door. He opens the heavy door, and he can see cold, grey concrete stairs, disappearing both upwards and downwards, flanked at the side by a railing that could be either wrought iron or stainless steel. Almost immediately as the door closes behind him he is overcome by a strange feeling of being invincible, cocooned in a casing of quietness and safety. The imaginary stairwell is providing him with another dimension where the receptionist in the waiting room and the security officers, who may occasionally patrol the corridor, cannot reach him.

He notices that a pale yellow-tinted light switched on automatically when he opened the door, but he guesses that it is worked by sensors and that it will soon turn off unless he keeps moving. He begins to descend the stairs, flight by flight, holding on to the railing as the descent is making him feel a little dizzy. Floor thirty-two. Floor twenty-eight.

His shoes are making a terrifying clattering sound on the hard stairs, so he removes them. Holding them in one hand he continues in his socks.

Floor twenty-one.

Floor nineteen.

Above the door to each floor there is a number, and he

is thankful that he is being kept updated as to where he is. When he reaches floor fifteen, he sits on the bottom step for a moment and rests.

Then he hears a door open somewhere above him. A moment later it slams shut.

Now he can hear footsteps on the stairs; whoever is above him is running down the stairs two at a time. He tries to open the door to floor fifteen, but it is obviously locked, and then he suddenly remembers that doors to emergency exit stairwells only open in one direction.

He looks around frantically. There is absolutely nowhere to hide in a stairwell, unless one happens to be a spider or a dust mite. The light is not fantastic but it is not so bad that he can simply fade into the shadows. He recognizes the undeniable fact that there is absolutely nowhere he can hide.

He closes his eyes, massages his forehead with his fingers and tries to expel the image of the stairwell. It is obvious that not even in his imagination is he permitted to escape.

While trying to dispel the image of the stairwell, he is also trying to rid himself of the idea that he would have considered removing his shoes and that he would then have continued down the stairs in his socks. He glances at his nicely polished brown lace-ups and feels relieved that they are still on his feet.

Arthur's pattern of routines and rituals is what holds him together, and it is the uncertainty into which he has been flung that is causing him so much distress. To cope, he always needs to know what is happening and the way in which it is happening. Nicely polished brown (or black or grey or even white) lace-ups are the only way in which feet should be presented; it is still worrying him that he should have even imagined himself walking anywhere in only socks.

He is thinking of the last time he saw his parents. It was about six months after the Change really came into force, and it must have been spring. He remembers that it was about seven or seven-thirty in the morning, and he and his parents were sitting at the table, having breakfast. Outside the window the wattle was in full bloom - hence his deduction that it must have been spring - and the sky was a soft blue colour. For some reason he remembers his mother saying that it was going to be a lovely day.

His brother was not at home. Arthur tries to remember why, but his memory as regards George is hazy, and he is unable to grab hold of the whole picture. He stops trying to search for the pieces and decides that because he and his parents were sitting at the table it must have been a Saturday, and no one was leaving the house early. He focuses on the tablecloth - blue with large yellow and orange flowers, that his mother had bought several years earlier in a sale, excited that the yellow in the cloth matched the yellow of her breakfast crockery - and his mind weaves around the patterns in the cloth and tests the weight of the stoneware mugs and the almost square plates. He cannot remember anything else that was on the table, but he does remember that he had made a connection between the yellow mugs and the wattle outside the window, deciding that the repetition of such a happy colour had to be positive.

But he was wrong.

He remembers that his father was pouring himself a second cup of coffee and his mother was spreading toast with red or yellow jam when there was a knock at the door.

Arthur had not been expecting anyone, and he did not believe that his parents were either - not so early in the morning. His parents looked at each other, and his father quickly glanced at his watch, an heirloom that he had received from his grandfather. Thinking back, Arthur wonders if he may have seen frowns crossing both their faces or whether this is a false memory that has been created by time. Arthur is certain that no one said anything, but he knew that a knock on the door so early in the day had to be a cause for worry.

Arthur's father put down the coffee pot, pushed back his chair, and walked to the front door.

Arthur remembers watching as his mother placed the knife, with which she had been spreading her toast, on the side of her plate. The yellow light of a perfect morning was suddenly tinged with something else, and Arthur was not sure which routine or ritual he should use to revert everything back to normal - back to the blue and yellow of the perfect morning.

He moved his plate to the centre of one of the yellow-orange flowers on the tablecloth and placed his mug near the top of the plate, close but not touching. He could not make up his mind whether the plate and the mug should be touching: perhaps 'touching' might tie everything together and make things safe; on the other hand, 'touching' might close off other possibilities and the likelihood of a happy outcome. The uncertainty was making Arthur anxious, but he could not decide what to do. He stood up and placed both his hands on the back of his chair. As long as he kept his hands on the chair, everything would be all right: the person at the door would go away, his father would return, and they would continue with their breakfast.

Arthur could hear his father talking with someone at

the door, but their voices were muffled, and he could not hear what was being said. His mother was already standing and was making a half-hearted attempt to collect together the things on the table, placing plates on top of each other with cutlery balanced on the very top. But, like Arthur, she was most probably also trying to pick up the conversation, so her packing was careful and relatively quiet. If she was aware of Arthur attempting to make things better by holding on to his chair, she did not say anything; perhaps she was prepared to accept any kind of magic if it really worked.

Arthur's father was on his way back to the kitchen. Arthur remembers his voice becoming clearer, louder, and he also remembers that there were other voices. He gripped the chair even harder.

As Arthur's father appeared at the kitchen door, he looked as though he was about to say something, but he was distracted by someone talking to him. Arthur could not see the person talking to his father: he wondered what he was saying and why. He began counting the orange flowers on the tablecloth. He could not see all of them, as the tablecloth hung down on all sides of the table, and the fact that he was unable to see all the flowers was worrying him. Should he walk around the table and count them properly, or should he simply be satisfied with an approximation? At this thought, Arthur shuddered: approximations were the worst thing he could imagine; it would be better not to count the flowers at all than to depend on an approximation.

Arthur remembers his father putting his hands on his shoulders and telling him to take care. His mother hugged him, and then the door opened and closed and, suddenly, they were both gone. Arthur became aware that he was still holding on to the chair: he was too terrified to let go.

The house was silent, and Arthur was alone.

Ten minutes later another number is read out. It belongs to a large middle-aged woman in a burgundy-coloured tent dress who is sitting at the far right of the first row of chairs. The grey-haired woman has most probably been sitting there for several hours, when the finality of the situation catches up with her, somewhat unexpectedly; she lets go of the thin veneer of self-control that has been keeping her relatively calm, and she falls apart into a multitude of small pieces. She lets go of everything that has been reinforcing her hope of some kind of reprieve or deliverance, and begins to scream.

And she continues screaming.

The people sitting closest to the woman look uncomfortable and concerned; should they comfort her? Should they tell her that everything is going to be all right when they have no way of knowing if it will be anything that is even close to 'right'? Even if they are certain that they are waiting for a medical appointment, they cannot know what news *she* is expecting once she passes through that door. Have they also been teetering on the same precipice from which she has obviously fallen? Are they now wondering which of them will be next?

Arthur thinks: Obviously she does not believe she is here for something ordinary like a health check. Or does she?

The person closest to the woman, an elderly gentleman with a walking stick in one hand, reaches out and touches her arm.

From the desk at the back of the room, the receptionist calls out loudly, '6134-194, go to the door immediately. Please remember that we must keep to the schedule.'

The woman who has the number 6134-194 carefully stitched on her dress is quickly moving beyond hysterical, and she no longer seems aware of anyone else in the room, least of all the receptionist.

The receptionist sighs loudly and impatiently; leaving her knitting and her PS on the desk, she makes her way noisily to the first row of chairs.

Like many others in the room, Arthur is overcome by anguish for the woman, which, if he is completely honest, is most probably a reflection on his own distress and apprehension. He is quite sure that he understands her paralysing fear - a fear that does not reason or think logically; a fear that explodes through the body, leaving no pockets of sanity. He glances around him: anyone in the room could be that woman. He and everyone else in the room have doubtlessly been concentrating on keeping themselves from the abyss, but it would take only the very slightest thought or image to push any of them over the edge.

He does not have to guess what it was that pushed the woman over the edge.

Like looking at a black-and-white film from a bygone era before sound, or staring at people moving on the other side of a large shop window, Arthur watches while the receptionist walks towards the woman. He is no longer part of the scene - he is simply an observer. He hears nothing, and the movements of those involved are dream-like, almost unreal. But he is not completely focused on the drama unfolding before him; part of his brain has once again begun to look at the possibility of escape - an area of thought that makes little sense if, as he hopes, there is something completely normal behind the waiting-room door.

The door to the corridor is not far from where he is sitting, but he already knows that it is automatically locked from the waiting-room side and that it can, there-fore, not be considered a feasible escape route. As he analyses the situation, while looking frantically around the room in the hope of seeing some other exit possibility that he may have previously missed, he becomes aware that someone must have turned up the sound several levels.

The sound of the woman's screams is shattering any equilibrium he may have had left.

The receptionist has now reached the row of chairs closest to the exit door and is severely reprimanding the burgundy-covered woman. She removes a communication device from her pocket, looking towards the entry door at the back of the room as she does so. For a short instant her eyes meet those of Arthur, and Arthur wonders if she is able to read his innermost thoughts that are so tied up with his overwhelming desire to escape.

She speaks softly into the device and then returns it to her pocket.

The large woman is holding on to the seat of her chair, with both hands clenched vice-like around its edge. Looking straight ahead with unseeing eyes, she is no longer screaming, but she is murmuring lines of nonsense to herself. Her blotched face is streaked with tears and strings of mucous, running from her nose, and she makes no attempt to wipe anything away. She may not have gone through the door, but she has exited into a place whence no one can follow her.

Arthur is disconcerted by everything that has been happening, by his realization that escape is probably out of the question, and by the fact that the receptionist looked at him. In his highly anxious state he wonders why she looked at *him* and not at someone else in the room, and he sits still for some time, his eyes fixed on the front wall, avoiding the door. He has not discovered any other exit from the room, or anything that vaguely resembles an exit. The walls are complete in their whiteness, unbroken except for the two doors - one leading into the room and one leading out of the room. Arthur's thoughts baulk at this point: he would really like to know what is on the other side of that door. Then he thinks that he may be getting himself into a state of anxiety for no reason at all; perhaps the door, like all waiting-room doors, leads to something normal and even mundane. He wonders if this time tomorrow, after his medical or his dental check-up, he will be thinking of how foolish he had been. The thought has barely passed through his mind before a tsunami of anxiety sweeps through him, pushing all reasonable, sensible thoughts ahead of it. He thinks: Perhaps there will be no tomorrow, at least not for me.

The imagery of his possible annihilation is not helping him at all, and after a few moments he consciously redirects his fear and apprehension towards the fact that he has been waiting so long. He checks the time on the clock behind him and thinks of all the things he could have been doing had he not been sitting in the waiting room.

His shift at the Department of Discarded and Lost Property would have finished at four. Thinking about the department and finishing his shift, he recollects that when he had contacted his supervisor that morning and asked for time off in the afternoon, no one had seemed surprised; in fact, it was almost as though everyone knew something that Arthur himself did not know. Was his supervisor party to the whole thing? Did he know why Arthur had been called to Building C? Could he have put Arthur out of his misery by making some remark about dentists or medicals or taxation? Or was he aware of something else that had absolutely nothing to do with health checks or paperwork?

Later, after returning home, he would have made himself a pot of Earl Grey tea, and he would have sat in the small kitchen with his tea and his PS. Arthur knew that the news on his personal screen was worse than useless - all news having been collected, edited, and communicated by the Party - but he enjoyed the feeling that he was doing something ordinary. It also conjured up memories of his father reading the newspaper at breakfast. Safe. Secure. Ordinary.

After his tea and his PS, he would most probably,

unless it was raining, have taken a walk to the nearby park, where he would have watched the pigeons and the mynah birds, all of them anxiously guarding their own invisibly marked territories. He would not have seen any children playing - children were rarely seen in such public places - but he may have seen the girl from the office, the girl with the short fair hair and the blue eyes. She was nearly always smiling, and, although Arthur found it difficult to understand why anyone would want to be smiling, things being the way they were, he appreciated her smiles, and he found himself looking forward to them. Occasionally, when he passed by her desk in the morning, he would stop and they would exchange a few words; sometimes they drank coffee together; several times they had met by chance in the park where they had laughed at the antics of the birds and walked around the moderately large man-made lake, carefully avoiding the marshy sections where water pooled among the green grasses.

Had they known each other before the Change, they may eventually have moved in with each other, had two or three children and settled down to a reasonably happy life together. Now, after the Change, things were not so simple.

Thinking about the girl with the fair hair makes him think of Rowena, and he wonders whether the girl from the office was simply an emotional replacement for Rowena. He stops at the word *replacement*: it has such an antiseptic feel about it. Is it possible to replace a person? he asks himself, and decides that it is not.

Arthur's thoughts move away from Rowena and the girl in the office and from what he might have been doing had he not been sitting in the waiting room, and they swing back to his earlier observation that, in reality, life is just one big waiting room. Thinking back to the dentist's waiting room of his childhood, he reflects that it is no wonder that there are so many people living in a constant state of anxiety. They are all waiting for something for which they would prefer not to be waiting.

There is a lot of noise behind him as the door from the corridor opens and loud, self-confident footsteps make their way to the reception desk where the receptionist is again sitting. He hears muffled talking, and then two security officers, carrying a stretcher, and a paramedic, carrying a medium-size hardside bag, walk to the front of the room where the woman in the burgundy dress is still in her own world, talking to herself.

The paramedic opens his bag, takes out a pre-filled hypodermic syringe, rolls back the woman's sleeve, wipes her arm with antiseptic, and carefully injects the contents of the syringe into her arm. During the entire procedure, the woman continues talking to herself and looking ahead, showing no awareness of the man or of what he is doing.

The two security officers then open up the stretcher

they have been carrying and, with an expertise that can only come from regular practice, lift the woman on to it. The three men and the woman leave the room through the door at the front of the room, with the paramedic, who has now returned the hypodermic to his bag, leading the way.

He met Rowena only weeks after his parents and brother disappeared. He had been at the local library, looking for something that might give him an answer or, at least, some form of solace, knowing all the time that what he was looking for did not exist, when he noticed a woman sitting in one of the study booths at the far side of the library. He probably would not have paid her any further attention, but he noticed that she was watching him.

He felt strangely uncomfortable as though he was wearing his shirt inside out, or was wearing mismatched shoes, or had forgotten his trousers. He gave himself a cursory glance and tried to concentrate on scanning the bookshelf in front of him. His curiosity, however, was too great, and when he quickly looked back in the direction of the woman, she was still looking at him.

Grabbing a couple of books from the shelf, he walked across the room. 'Have we met?' he asked, wondering if she was perhaps someone from his short time at Teachers' College or whether he had met her somewhere else.

She shook her head, a small smile playing around her mouth. 'I don't think so,' she said, as she closed the book in front of her.

Arthur frowned a little and adjusted his glasses.

The woman held out her hand, looked around her and said softly, 'Rowena. My name's Rowena.'

Rowena came into Arthur's life at the same time as numbers were replacing names, and people were being moved into other forms of housing and other careers. Like so many others, Arthur felt that he was losing control, but at the same time he was beginning to feel that he could no longer cope, being alone in the house with its enormous volume of memories and accusations. Perhaps if he had been more unconventional: organized his books, or even his clothes, according to a different mathematical equation; got up at 6.30 or 4.20 or 7.05 instead of 6.15; eaten his toast before his cereal; then perhaps he would still be living with his family in the house at the edge of the town. He was almost sure that everything that happened was completely dependent on what he had or had not done. In his mind, George's disappearance, only days after that last breakfast with his parents, confirmed this. He believes that he may have had a chance to do things differently, but he had been paralysed with fear, and he had done nothing. He had changed nothing. He had remained in his room with the blinds down, thinking of the blue and yellow kitchen, the sun streaming in through the window and how his parents had said goodbye and had still not returned.

He thought a lot about the voices he had heard, wondering who owned them and what connection they had had with his parents. When his brother also disappeared, he did not have to guess what had happened to him; he knew that the same people were somehow involved.

He had briefly considered going to the police, but he had no way of knowing if the voices he had heard could have belonged to the police. Things were changing so rapidly around him, and he was unable to get his head into a space where he could devise new routines and new formulas. He was completely vulnerable; if he had had more time, he could probably have set up some safeguards, and he may have been able to prevent it all from happening.

Rowena tried to assure him that there was an explanation for everything and that things that seemed negative on the surface may not be negative at all. She was sure that there was a reason why his parents and his brother had gone away, and she was equally sure that they would eventually return. He did not agree with everything that she said, but she had a calming effect on him, and within only a matter of months she had moved in with him in the house on the edge of the town.

Arthur is uncomfortably aware just how much the entire episode with the large woman has upset him. He closes his eyes for a moment to shut out the light, the images of the three men and the woman, and the room itself. With his eyes closed, he pretends for a moment that he is completely blind. If he were blind, he could disappear into his own world: he would not have to worry about all the things going on around him. The sensation of nothingness, which is composed of neither blackness nor an absence of blackness, is restful, but his 'blindness' is only voluntary, and, when he opens his eyes again, he can see the room, the walls, the people, and, in front of him, the door.

Probably because of the disquieting episode with the woman, he is not only more anxious but also feels that he is in danger of losing the last remnants of control he may still have. The woman has given voice to what Arthur imagines is something that everyone in the room is trying to suppress. He could easily follow her over the top, but for his own sake he needs to retain some form of self-control. Whether he walks through that door himself, or whether, like the woman, he is carried out of the waiting room on a stretcher, the final result will still be the same.

It just does not make any sense; but then, he wonders, does anything about his life in general or the waiting room in particular make sense?

Arthur is looking around the room again. He focuses on the white walls and then on the door at the front of the room. His seeing and feeling capacities are no longer part of the entity he regards as *Arthur* but more like something encapsulated in a container with the name Arthur emblazoned on the side. He feels as though he is two separate people or beings: the one on the outside that everyone can see and the one on the inside that no one can see, not even himself. But what is it that comprises this thing, this organism called Arthur or 7891-447? Is it his appearance, his thoughts, his feelings, his fears? Arthur moves his eyes around the door, noting the colour variations and the contrast between the brown of the door and the white of the walls. Everything is a matter of contrasts, he decides - good and bad, black and white, happy and sad.

As a child, Arthur had never given much thought to Unitas - it is unlikely that he even knew what it was - but, thinking back, he remembers hearing conversations between his parents and people who extolled the virtues of the new political party, expressed guarded concern, or, as was often the case, showed no interest whatsoever. By the time Arthur was well into his teens, and Unitas was suddenly a major part of everyone's reality, people were becoming much more polarized: a majority claimed that Unitas was the best thing that had happened for several decades, if not centuries, while a minority feared that it was an organization with a hidden agenda. Society had been in the process of a radical transformation for some time, and now, as Unitas took control, it became obvious that it was too late to take a step backwards. Individual thought had been more or less whittled away as the majority latched on to causes, ideas, phrases, and even suggestions, without discrimination; they had learnt to like or dislike in accordance with the dictates of those around them.

When the Change finally took place, it happened so subtly and so efficiently that no one was aware of anything out of the ordinary until that moment when the balance tipped. Arthur can still remember how the elation and joy of the many slowly turned to dismay, confusion, and self-accusation. Suddenly, there was so much self-reproach: where had they gone wrong? Why had they not seen what had been happening right in front of them? What could they have done to have stopped it?

A number of people - both original protesters and others who had finally woken up to what was happening - raised their voices and objected. But their voices were too weak when compared with the growing confidence and the power of the movement. There was nothing that anyone could do now when everything was already in place. When Arthur thought back on it all, he reluctantly admitted to himself that, for whatever reason, the majority was completely content with the new government. Most people saw no reason to change what had been more or less flung upon them: they felt that someone, finally, was in control.

Arthur wondered then, as he still wonders, how people could have been so unbelievably gullible and how they had been able to miss all the obvious signs. It irritates him that people could lose the capacity to think either independently or analytically - they were all like herd animals, mindlessly following the one in front. In his mind he could see the banner-carrying Unitas leader followed by a never-ending line of cows - brown, red-brown, white, black, mottled, beige - all of them obediently following the cow in front; none of them reflecting on the fact that the grass to the left or the right might be greener or that the small track on the left might in fact lead to a freer, more independent, life. He stops in his train of thought and wonders if it is even possible for a cow to have an independent life. The imagery is possibly all wrong, but, even then, before Unitas had become the force it now is, he had resented the loss of his freedom and his future, and he is understandably both frustrated and angry.

Arthur's thoughts move away from the images of cows as he ponders the fact that most people probably had no reason to suspect anything: they were simply looking for security and a better way of life. Perhaps they had been too trusting, too passive, too turned off. In the early years when he discussed these ideas with Rowena, she had told him that he was misreading the entire situation. There was nothing particularly sinister about Unitas, she had said on more than one occasion; no government is perfect - they all have their own agendas, and some agendas are better or worse than others. She agreed that people had had no reason to suspect anything but that was because there was nothing to suspect.

However, Arthur was not convinced. He knew that there was something intrinsically evil about Unitas, and it amazed him that others could not see what, to him, was blatantly obvious. It also amazed him how, in an age where communication and global connection were the cement that held everything together, any movement, political or otherwise, could gain complete and utter supremacy. He found it ludicrous when there were so many checks in place. Or were there? Arthur was no longer so sure. Obviously the checks had not worked, and once Unitas was in control of the communication and connection networks, it was completely and unrestrictedly in control of everything.

Some of the people who raised their voices against the new government did so only for a very short period of time. It was very obvious to Arthur that Unitas was not going to tolerate any kind of protest, and it made sense to him, in a macabre way, that those who persisted quickly disappeared. He could understand that no one wanted to disappear, and it was therefore logical that everyone, reluctantly or otherwise, accepted that life for them was going to be very different to what it had been in the past.

Arthur closes his eyes. He wants to completely negate the bright light and the physical reality of the waiting room. Were he able to read, the light would probably not be a problem; in fact, it would be a definite advantage. But he is not permitted to read, and therefore, bored with the long wait and the almost sterile room, his imagination is seeking out its own entertainment. With his eyes closed, he tries to force his imagination into believing that he is somewhere else, somewhere far away from Building C, but his imagination does not want to be forced, and it breaks free, creating its own images and its own realities.

He has passed through the door at the front of the room, and he is immediately confronted by a corridor with timber flooring and white walls. The ceiling is bisected lengthways by thin light tubes and there is a large black arrow on the wall in front of him. It is obvious from the layout of the corridor that there is only one direction for him to choose, so he finds the arrow both superfluous and irritating.

At the end of the corridor there is a lift.

Even though part of his brain is fully aware that he is seated on an aqua plastic chair in a white-walled waiting room, his anxiety and sense of vulnerability are climbing to new heights. The image of the confined corridor, completely devoid of people, is pushing away any logical thoughts he may have had, and he can see himself walking slowly along the short corridor in the direction of the arrow. His imagination is not giving him a preview of what may be ahead of him; although he is somehow aware that he could simply open his eyes and dispel all the images, something inside of him is urging him towards the lift. Perhaps the lift will give him the answer he has been searching for.

He stares at the corridor and is thankful that he is still alive.

While he thinks about being alive, he is also very aware of all the things he has imagined waiting for him on the other side of the door. None of them have eventuated, but he is not quite sure whether he should continue being thankful or not; he has no way of knowing what to expect when he reaches the lift.

With his eyes tightly shut, he watches himself as he continues walking towards the lift. Terrified by all the imagined possibilities of what might be awaiting him in the lift, he knows that if he is to avoid a panic attack it is crucial that he can stifle his anxiety, so, even in his imagination, he forces himself to think of other things: the orange concrete building where he has lived for the past fifteen years or so, and the other people in the waiting room.

Someone had once said to Arthur, many years ago, that we create our own realities and that it is completely up to us whether our realities are positive or negative. Every happening, every event, every thought has a plus side and a minus side. It is a simple law of nature - yin and yang, dark and light, fire and water. We choose, one side or the other, not always consciously but always motivated by a myriad other factors. Most of the time we are not even aware whether our choice is more to one side than the other, and when things seem to go in the wrong direction we blame Fate or God or the political situation.

At the time, Arthur felt that although some of it made sense he did not feel that he was able to agree with everything, but as the years tumbled past, one after the other, and the Change became *the* reality, he was no longer completely certain that it was possible to have an own, individually tailored reality. Standing in the lift as it sinks into the bowels of the building, he begins to wonder if perhaps he may have misunderstood what the person was trying to make him understand all those years ago. The Change really had nothing to do with it. In many ways the Change was simply a superficial part of his life: his reality was how he managed to relate to the world into which he had been thrown.

He focuses on the fact that, in his imagination at least, he is in the lift. He knows that he must have entered it - the doors must have opened, and he must have stepped inside - but he has no memory of doing so. While he grapples with the concept of being somewhere and not knowing how he got there, he is also aware that dreams and daydreams and even imagination do not necessarily follow ordinary rules and regulations. In real life, Arthur knows that he must activate the control pad to open the lift door, that he must then walk through that door and possibly even activate another control pad inside the lift.

While he is musing on how he arrived in the lift, he

becomes aware that the lift has come to a standstill. He has not even noticed that it has stopped, before the doors slide back and he sees that he is in what looks like the basement. In front of him there is what could have been an enormous underground parking station, pre-Change, but there are no cars, and definitely no hovers; the space is completely empty. There is a coldness emanating from the concrete walls and the pillars that break up the space at regular intervals and which, to Arthur, appear as man-made, regularly formed and regularly spaced, tree trunks. Although it seems ridiculous to think such a thing, he feels the weight of the building pressing down on the pillars and pressing down on him.

He stands outside the lift, surveying the space in front of him, wondering what is likely to happen next. He remembers the arrow in the corridor, and he inspects the wall closest to him, expecting to discover another arrow or, at least, instructions as to what he is to do next. There is nothing. He is aware that he is both anxious and exhausted to the point of collapse, and he scrutinizes the space in the hope of seeing somewhere where he might be able to sit down.

There is nowhere.

He tries to summon up the image of a comfortable chair, a mattress, or even one of the aqua plastic chairs, but his imagination refuses to comply, and he is left standing in the space, trying to decide if he will be able to sit on the cold, hard concrete floor. He thinks back to the emergency exit stairwell and the image of himself without shoes; he is not sure what would be worse - running down stairs without shoes or sitting on the concrete floor of a parking station.

He remembers that he has not eaten since he took a very hurried lunch before leaving work, but the level of his anxiety is making the thought of food repulsive. Even in this parallel world, his stomach is in a constant state of turbulence; though he is used to eating at set times, he doubts that he would be able to keep any food down at the moment. On the other hand, he would not say no to a cup of strong coffee, and he really needs some water. He wonders how long it takes to become completely de-hydrated, and whether it is a painful, stressful process or whether one simply slips into a state of unconsciousness. A second quick glance around the space does not reveal any taps and especially no water dispensers, but the space is vast and it is possible that there is a tap on the far side.

He tries to imagine a tap, a water dispenser, a bubbler, a water fountain, a table with cold drinks - small wet droplets forming on the outside of the glasses - but the images fail to take shape, and quickly break up and disappear.

The magnitude of the basement together with the silence is beginning to get on his nerves. On some level, he knows that all he has to do is to open his eyes, but he wants to find out more; he wants answers. This is not what he had expected; he had expected something bad but not quite like this. He wonders where everyone could be hiding, or perhaps there have never been people this far down in the building. The absence of people is worrying him more than anything else.

Something tells him that he should keep moving, and he watches while the figure that is himself sets off to walk around the space. He is hoping to find a tap or, at least, somewhere to sit, and he feels very small in the large space, his footsteps echoing around him. At the far side of the space, having found neither a tap nor anywhere to sit, he finally sits down on the floor, leaning back against the wall. He is totally exhausted; there is no point pushing himself any further.

Arthur sees himself slump against the hard, cold concrete, his mind slipping into a place that is squashed between anxiety, consciousness and sleep.

He opens his eyes, the image of the parking station still intact somewhere at the back of his mind, while his thoughts begin to wander back over his life. He thinks: isn't this what happens when one is about to die? He does not want to die; he does not want to think of his past, but he is too exhausted to stop his thoughts from running away from him.

Has there been anything in his life that was worthwhile? Did he achieve anything? Does he have regrets?

He regrets losing Rowena. Had she continued to be part of his life, he may have avoided some of the stress and unhappiness that has consistently plagued him; he may have even avoided the waiting room and whatever it is that is beyond the waiting room. She was always the sane, logical part of the relationship, while he was invariably focused on other things - the accumulated routines and practices that he believed he needed to get him through the day. He thinks of her short light-brown hair that never sat exactly the way she wanted it to, her blue eyes, and her smile. It was her smile that he missed most of all, especially now, thinking back. He imagines what it would be like should Rowena be sitting next to him in the waiting room. She would stretch out and take hold of his hand; her hand would be smooth and cool to the touch, and he would feel her confidence and her closeness. She would probably squeeze his hand, just a little, and smile at him, and her smile would make him believe that there was absolutely nothing to worry about. She would know what to do - she always knew what to do - and she would know a way out. He thinks again - had Rowena still been with him, they would never have ended up in a place like the waiting room.

He is bitter that Unitas took over his life: he is sad that he lost his family, and he has never really adjusted to living in a unit in a tower block. In between thinking about all the big disappointments and all the small annoyances,

Arthur is aware of glimpses of other things - walks around the lake, sunrises and sunsets, the girl at work, the comforting warmth of his Earl Grey tea.

Then he remembers something from earlier in the afternoon. The large open space. He was daydreaming or simply letting his imagination run riot, and he is sure that it had something to do with what he imagined could be behind the waiting room door. Slowly the image becomes clearer as all the pieces slide together: he believes that the space may have been a warehouse, or, on the other hand, it could simply have been a very wide open space. He can remember wondering what it was used for and why it was completely empty. Now he recollects that there were windows, and when he looked out of one of the windows—

His train of thought stops suddenly as he thinks again of the parking space: there are no windows in the parking space. Then he shakes his head, thinking how ridiculous he is being, looking for correlations between what is, in essence, two different dreams. Without consciously trying to resurrect his thoughts, he remembers what he had been thinking about earlier: something about realities and the choices we make, but he is too exhausted to give it much consideration, and he concentrates on emptying his mind of all thoughts.

Although he has been sitting in the waiting room for so many hours, he has not been able to adjust himself to the restricting nature of the room - the white walls, the lack of windows, the minimalist furnishings and the bright, almost unpleasant light. Every so often he closes his eyes, but he finds it difficult to keep them closed for any length of time - being able to see what is going on around him is the only form of control he has left.

While part of his mind is contemplating the room, the light, and the uncomfortable chair, the other part is still trying to work out why he should have been brought to the room in the first place. He cannot remember having been due for any kind of health check, nor can he remember having made any other kind of appointment. He knows that it is almost time for him to renew his PB, but he has no recollection of having made such an appointment, and even had he done so he cannot imagine that it would require a wait of several hours.

The PB - Personal Band or Bracelet, depending on one's gender - is a black stainless steel band one centimetre wide that is worn on either the left or the right wrist. As well as containing a GPS tracking device, the PB contains a wealth of information about the wearer - his or her health record, level of education, qualifications, employment history, psychological profile, police reports, travel history - and gives him or her access to the driverless buses and trains and, in other sectors, ferries, which are the main forms of transport. The PB is also linked to the wearer's bank account and is used for all payments or money transfers - money as a physical entity no longer exists. Once children reach the age of three, they are issued with their PB, and it is usually checked and replaced every second year. It fits reasonably snugly on to the wrist and it cannot be removed; any attempt to cut it off would instigate an alarm. Arthur has always resented his PB, but there is very little he can do about it.

Somewhere in the back of his mind, there is an image trying to push its way to the front. He is not sure if the image is worth looking at, but as it moves closer and closer to the front of his mind, he begins to wonder if it could perhaps be the answer to one of his questions.

It was two or three weeks ago, and he was enjoying his designated morning coffee break at the Department of Discarded and Lost Property. Coffee breaks are always staggered, which means that the majority of the work-force is always working at any given time. Productivity is the goal; they are not employed to drink coffee.

On this particular day, while Arthur was in the small

recreation room, drinking his coffee, he could hear people moving around the arena-like sorting area; he could hear boxes being taped and boxes being moved; he could hear muted voices; and, although he could not hear the actual process taking place, he could visualize lists of items being recorded to the many computing devices.

They were three workers having a coffee break. While they were enjoying the few precious minutes of not having to do anything in particular, their eyes kept darting to the large digital clock with the black digits. One of the men was several years older than Arthur but the third was little more than a boy. Arthur guessed that this was most probably the boy's first job.

It was also not difficult to work out that the boy with the close-cropped haircut and the pimples had only ever known the Unitas version of society, which he was going to great lengths to praise.

Arthur had woken late that morning, and, as a result, had missed breakfast, bungled a number of his routines, and had taken a wrong turn on his way to work. He was understandably not in a particularly good mood, and for whatever reason - no doubt fuelled by the serious deviation from his normal routine - he took a marked dislike to the boy: he disliked his appearance; he disliked his over-confident manner; he particularly disliked his opinions. He said: 'You know, things weren't always like this.'

The boy put down his empty cup, looked directly at

Arthur, his head on one side, grinned, and prompted, 'Worse, no doubt?'

Arthur said: 'Don't know if I'd say that. From what I remember, things were much better before— '

The other, older, man looked at Arthur pointedly.

The boy said nothing.

There is a worrying finality about the whole process - the letter, the building, the waiting room, the door - and Arthur does not like the word *final*, even though he is quite certain that *final* is what this charade is all about. They could have collected him at his flat; they could have wrapped him into a straitjacket, thrown him into an ambulance or a van and driven him to wherever they wanted, but the letter and the waiting room and the hours of anxiety have accentuated his fear by pushing the finality further into the future. Giving him hope when there is none to be had. Although the logic seems to be against him, he has not given up hoping that he has got it all wrong and that he really did have an appointment with some ordinary professional. If, on the other hand, his gut feeling is right, then he is hoping that he might be able to discover a sliver of a chance to escape or that they will suddenly change their minds and let him go.

And *they* have most probably known all along that such a sliver simply does not exist.

While knowing that Unitas must have some method of dealing with dissenters, Arthur veers away from the idea that unacceptable opinions could lead to execution. Unitas might be everyone's nightmare, but, for Arthur, execution is such a foreign concept and so very past tense that he simply cannot get his head around either the possibility or the probability.

Were dissenters taken out to sea and drowned? Were they shot? Were they locked away in specially constructed gaols? Or were they subjected to mind-changing surgery? Arthur has heard so many different rumours, and although he has pondered and analysed he has refused to believe any of them, interpreting most of what he has heard as mere reflections of people's fear. As long as he refuses to believe, then there is a chance that the rumours will remain rumours and will not become real. Arthur knows that once something is given an authentic label, it becomes a fact. But, while others outline their theories and he shakes his head and smiles incredulously, he knows that *something* has to happen to all the people who disagree: none of them are around any more - they have all disappeared.

And now there is a strong possibility that he is one of these people.

Arthur is aware that Unitas reallocates people between

sectors, cancels and changes careers, professions, training courses, and employment options, and keeps itself updated as to who is doing what and, quite likely, who is thinking what. People who are deemed a threat to the system, like Arthur, are moved to areas where they are less threatening and where the chance of their mounting some opposition or rebellion is unlikely. That is how Arthur found himself at the Department of Discarded and Lost Property. He had been devastated; he had complained; he had written letters; he had even pleaded with the principal of the teachers' college to intercede on his behalf. The principal, knowing full well that his power to intercede on anyone's behalf had been removed, and knowing that his own career hung perilously in the balance, shook his head sadly. There was absolutely nothing that he could do.

At first Arthur hated everything about the Department of Discarded and Lost Property, but eventually he realized that this was going to be his life and that he had no choice but to make the best of it. He could have ended up in any number of much worse places - he knew of people who were now working for the Department of Environment and Beautification and who spent their days sorting rubbish.

He should never have let himself be irritated by the boy. If only it were possible to replace the reality of his *now* with what had been before.

For some reason, his thoughts insist on returning to images of the parking station. He wonders if the images are trying to tell him something - he has heard of people who have psychic powers and are able to foretell the future and explain the past. Perhaps he has such powers and perhaps there actually is such a parking space in a basement somewhere beneath the waiting room.

While thinking about the parking station, he is also becoming more and more aware that he is extremely thirsty. He is finding it difficult to focus on anything: images, thoughts, sounds. Everything is blurring together. In his mind, he scans the area that resembles a parking station, but the effort of trying to work out what is real and what is embedded in his imagination is becoming too difficult.

He must have something to drink.

He is back in the parking station, lying on the concrete floor, and he believes that there is someone standing next to him. He stretches out his arm, sweeping it in a wide, but fairly erratic, arc, without touching anyone. His brain is telling him that there is no one there; it is also trying to tell him that the parking space is not real. Something else is telling him that someone is tapping him on the shoulder.

For some unknown reason, it makes sense to Arthur that someone should be tapping him on the shoulder. Perhaps the tapping has some connection with his future, limited or otherwise. He pulls himself up into a sitting position and thinks: it must be the middle of the night.

Is he awake or is he asleep? Is he sitting up, or is he simply imagining that he is sitting up? Is he imagining that he is imagining himself in the empty space? Is there really a man in a white coat standing next to him, or is he also part of his imagination within his imagination? Is he conversing with himself asleep or awake? Arthur is too exhausted to worry.

'I am so sorry. *So* very, very sorry,' the man is saying.

Arthur wonders why he is sorry. As far as he knows, he has not done anything for which he should be sorry. If anyone should be sorry it is Arthur. He is sorry that his life has been such a mess: his parents, George, Rowena, his studies. Everything. He is also sorry that he has been sitting for hours in an unpleasant waiting room, and he is also sorry that - in his imagination at least - he is now in what appears to be a parking station, sitting on a cold concrete floor without anything to drink.

The man is saying something about being held up and how he should have been there when Arthur arrived. Arthur reflects on the strangeness of having a character in his head with whom he is carrying on a conversation. Or perhaps it is more correct to say that the character is doing the talking and Arthur is merely listening. He wonders if it is the right word to use: is it possible to listen to someone who is not real but who is merely—

The man interrupts his train of thought, 'I mean, what did you think, arriving in a place like this, and no one at all to welcome you or to explain anything. As I said, I am so sorry—'

People who imagine that they hear voices are considered to be mentally unstable, Arthur thinks without opening his eyes. Obviously he has reached that point where everything is about to disintegrate. A bit like the woman in the burgundy dress. Everyone disintegrates in different ways: some people scream, others rip off their clothes and run around naked. He obviously slips off into parallel universes where he hears voices and communicates with unseen people.

Is it a mirage, a dream, a parallel reality? Arthur really does not know. He is also not sure where the borders are any longer - the borders between what he perceives to be real and what cannot possibly be real.

He does not want to open his eyes.

He concentrates on where he is, sitting on an uncomfortable chair in a claustrophobic waiting room. But the image of the parking space refuses to leave him. He remembers all those things he has heard about people who can visualize the future; people who can push their thoughts beyond what is now into a place that has yet to eventuate. Perhaps he is one of those people? Why otherwise would the same images keep re-occurring; why are so many of his thoughts in a space he has never inhabited in reality? He accepts the fact that he is anxious and worried and that anxiety can push the mind in strange directions, but he also accepts the possibility that his mind - so much more far-reaching than his physical self - may be trying to tell him something. He thinks of the stairwell that led nowhere, of the enormous warehouse-like expanse, and the windows looking out on to an unconnected area, and, now, the parking space. He knows there is a connection, but he is unable to find it. As his conscious mind begins to sift through all the bits and pieces, placing them in different patterns, the hollow feeling of anxiety overwhelms his body.

The man is still talking to him; Arthur, discarding the puzzle pieces, interrupts him, saying, 'And you are?'

The man is blurred, but Arthur can see that he looks slightly distracted, probably because he was interrupted mid-sentence, and although he looks as though he could easily say how sorry he is - again - he says, '4592-003.' He stretches out his hand to Arthur, who, on one of his planes of being, has heaved himself to his feet and is now standing.

In another part of his mind, Arthur asks himself if he felt that handshake. Was it warm, cold, limp, strong?

The man says, 'I'm here to answer your questions and see you on your way, so to speak.'

Arthur can feel the blood from his face rushing elsewhere in his body, and he thinks that he was evidently right all along. He decides that this is most likely the final phase, the last step before annihilation.

'It's a dreadful place.' 4592-003 waves his arms around what, for Arthur, is still an old-fashioned parking station. 'We usually meet clients on level twenty-four, but I was told to come down here. I was up on twenty-four, and then they said that there was a change of plan. No idea why, but that's the way it goes at times. You can never be completely sure of anything in life - you know, that bit about death and taxes.' He smiles at Arthur and adds, 'But you've probably heard that before?'

The physical Arthur, who has been sitting in the waiting room for hours; the official 7891-447; or even the Arthur who is caught somewhere in an enigmatic and confusing place that might be his future but, then again, might be someone else's past, really does not feel even remotely like smiling. He wishes that 4592-003 would get to the point.

'They really need to put in a few chairs or benches down here; it is most inhospitable that customers have to sit on the ground. I mean, look at the place. Once again, I do apologize.' 4592-003 looks genuinely concerned, and Arthur appreciates the thought even though he also wonders how it would help him, standing as he is on the springboard about to fling himself into oblivion.

The man checks some information on his PS and, looking up at Arthur, says, '7891-447?'

Arthur nods his head.

'Not fitting in that well? Anything you want to talk about? They've got you down here as a 635; that probably doesn't mean much to you, does it?' He manages something that is halfway between a laugh and an apology and switches screen.

Arthur is wondering if 635 means that he is about to be shot or beheaded. He is not too keen on 4592-003 carrying out either of these ghastly executions; he manages a very small smile as an image of 4592-003 raising his axe while apologising profusely floats across his mind.

He says, '635? Should I be concerned?'

4592-003 shakes his head, and then he purses his lips and says, 'Well, I suppose it depends. It's strange, I've never had that actual question before.' He looks directly at Arthur.

The two Arthurs, both the external and the internal, wonder if he is about to start apologizing all over again.

'A 635 is a transfer,' the man in the white coat explains. 'Actually, we use the same number for all transfers; it would make more sense to have different numbers for different types of transfers. But that's hardly of any interest to you?'

Arthur is trying to work out what could be meant by the word *transfer*. Is it possibly a euphemism for something more sinister? Perhaps he is about to be transferred from one state to another, less animated, state. Or perhaps it is simply a transfer with the meaning relocation. At least relocation would mean that he would most probably be able to keep his head. He is trying to think positively, but the last twelve hours have disturbed his ability to think logically - he has not even had his normal routines to hold on to and to keep him safe. The more he thinks about his routines and the ambiguity of the word *transfer,* the more he feels like screaming, or, at the very least, collapsing to the floor in a paralytic heap.

He opens his eyes, hoping to dispel all the images, but the parking space and the man remain before his mind. The little man seems unaware of Arthur's inner turmoil. He is still looking at his PS. He taps in some information, and then he looks at Arthur and says, 'Well, that's about it; I suppose we'd best be moving.'

Arthur would like to ask where to, but something inside of him says it is probably best that he does not know. He massages his head with his fingers while he thinks about coffee, the implications of hearing voices, and the idea that all that is between him and his future is a door in a white wall.

As the reception desk is directly behind him, he can easily hear the receptionist speaking with a new client. Client, patient, customer? He is not quite sure of the correct word. Because there is nothing much else to concentrate on, he finds himself automatically drawn to the conversation. He listens attentively, as, up until then, except during the incident with the hysterical woman, he has not heard the receptionist say much more than 'Number?' and 'Sit down'. He is interested by the fact that she is putting together several words into a sentence; moreover, she sounds particularly angry, so something out of the ordinary must have happened to have upset her.

He moves slightly in his chair and throws a glance over his left shoulder. There is a woman standing near the reception desk; she is wearing a long green woollen coat, and over one shoulder she is carrying a large colourful patchwork bag.

He turns his head back towards the front of the room, and sharpens his ears. The image of the woman remains firmly at the centre of his mind. Although he has only seen her for a matter of seconds, he is aware that she is tall and attractive and that her thick brown hair has been pulled back from her face in an untidy plait. From the ongoing conversation, he is almost certain that the commotion has something to do with the patchwork bag.

While he is listening to the argument at the other side of the room, he tries to place all the sentences into some kind of order; he approaches it as a jigsaw that must be laid or a puzzle that must be solved. Perhaps the girl - he is now almost certain that the female standing at the receptionist's desk is not much older than twenty-three or twenty-four - has misunderstood the 'bring nothing with you' bit, or perhaps her letter contained completely different instructions to his letter, or perhaps she cannot read.

At this point he realizes that he is being ridiculous, and the pieces of the jigsaw fly in different directions across his mind. Of course the girl can read; otherwise she would not have known to come to the waiting room on the thirty-sixth floor.

'But it's my *bag*,' the girl is saying to the receptionist, 'I don't go anywhere without it.'

Without turning around, he imagines the receptionist holding on to the bag while trying to prise it away from the girl. He would really like to be able to do something, but he has absolutely no idea as to what that might be. He is both stressed and concerned about the girl, but his concern for himself is greater.

He tries to convince himself that there is only one thing on which he should focus and that is the task he has been set: 'Present yourself at reception on the thirty-sixth floor.'

He is not sure what the consequences might be if he were to go to the girl's aid, but he cannot imagine them being at all positive. The likelihood of his being able to help her is not at all great; in fact, his getting involved would almost certainly make things worse for them both. She is already doing a pretty good job of messing things up for herself, and he really cannot see any sense in messing things up for himself as well.

The girl finally sits down on the chair recently vacated by a man who has been called to the door some half an hour earlier. The chair is only a couple of chairs from Arthur, and he looks across at her and smiles in a way that he hopes is encouraging, though, as soon as he has done it, he wonders what is encouraging about the situation in which they now find themselves.

She acknowledges his smile with a look that is a mixture of frustration and hopelessness. Although the look is brief, Arthur feels a vague contact with the woman, and he knows that had the situation been different he would have tried to help her. He would have *wanted* to help her. He catches himself up at this point, acutely aware of the enormous gulf between wanting something and being able to realize it.

He understands that the episode with the receptionist must have rattled her completely. He had seen how her thin hands were shaking, and if her hands were shaking then her entire body must be in a state of uproar. He guesses that her bag has most probably not been moved from the reception desk, but he does not want to give the receptionist the satisfaction of seeing him turn around to look.

It is bad enough being forced to come to a place like this in the first place, without being treated like some kind of imbecile. He feels extremely sorry for her; when he looks across at her a second time, he notices that she is now sitting on her hands, possibly in an attempt to stop them from shaking. Looking at her, he can imagine that she is probably still thinking of her bag, which is lying only a few metres behind her.

He wonders if she is kind-hearted; Arthur has decided that kindness is one of the only things that means any-thing, things being what they are; there are so many unkind people everywhere since the Change. He under-stands that everyone is desperately trying to place him- or herself in a positive light in a climate where the individual is no longer of any importance. He shakes his head, sending the thoughts about kindness and unkindness in different directions. He is reading far too much into a hasty glance. Perhaps she is like most other people: self-centred and afraid.

But, for some reason, Arthur's thoughts refuse to leave the image of the girl. She reminds him of someone he remembers seeing in his mid-twenties. It was shortly after he had moved into his flat, and he had seen her outside the purchase centre. It was a Thursday evening, his allocated evening for shopping; as he came out of the centre with his several bags of shopping, she was standing on the footpath. At first Arthur noticed her no more or no less than did all the other people going in and out of the centre, but then he saw that she was obviously upset, and that she had been crying.

Later, he felt that he should have gone up to her and asked her what was the matter, but he did nothing of the kind. He merely watched her for a few minutes, and then walked away. He recognized her anguish; he had felt it himself so many times. At first, he took it for granted that she may have been depressed and lonely, fighting against a system that she was unable to fathom and could not change, but then he considered the possibility that he may have been imagining things, and that he may have been painting a picture that reflected his anxieties and not hers. Perhaps she was upset for some other reason entirely, and even if he wanted to do something, he had no way of knowing what he should do, so it was easiest to simply walk away.

He rarely thought of her, but now the memory came rushing back at him, pinning him to his chair, taking away his breath. *He could have done something: he could have talked to her*. He takes another look at the girl with the long brown plait and thinks that she is very similar in appearance to the girl outside the purchase centre. He had not helped *her*, but if it is in any way possible he knows that he will try to help this girl.

He wonders why the receptionist was so noisily irritated. He doubts that the bag in itself could have caused such an outburst - there must have been something else. Arthur racks his brain, trying to work out why the woman, nasty at best, has suddenly become so belligerent. He has nothing else to do, and the mental exercise keeps his thoughts away from death and doors and the importance of light.

He decides that the letter the girl must have received would have been no less obscure than anyone else's, but she obviously missed the bit about not bringing anything with her. Although Arthur has no definite reason for suspecting that the girl has arrived late, he wonders if, as well as missing the bit about personal belongings, she may have also got the time wrong. Having moved off on that tangent, he pictures her leaving home late and then getting lost among the confusion of administration buildings. There are so many similar-looking buildings and entrances, and it is not impossible that she may have been stressed and bewildered and that time simply slipped away from her.

Or that may not be at all what happened. Arthur has no way of knowing; he is simply making a guess. Nevertheless, if she has arrived later than expected, Arthur feels that that could well be sufficient to upset the receptionist's very fragile equilibrium.

In a place where several very tall high-rise towers form a hub; where people receive official letters in mid-grey envelopes; where no one asks questions, and where, even if they were to do so, no one receives any answers; and where everything runs like clockwork, not only to the minute but to the second, any deviation from the strict routine can plunge the people in charge, if not the whole system, into chaos.

He sighs and rolls his shoulders, arching his back and feeling how the muscles around his neck have once again knotted themselves. As he does so, he moves his gaze around the room, marvelling at the fact that very few people are talking. It is not so strange that no one is reading, seeing that no one has access to a PS.

Thinking about whiling away the time, his thoughts move off on a tangent, and he remembers reading that it was once common, many years ago, for people to burn tobacco and then inhale the smoke. The article focused on all the unwanted side-effects, but it also mentioned that smoking was purported to eliminate stress. Arthur wonders if smoking had been able to help him in his present situation.

The evening drags on through a heavy haze of boredom, discomfort, and anxiety. The idea that boredom and anxiety could be thrown together as part of the same experience fascinates Arthur, but he is living proof that it is possible, and he swings between feeling totally fed up with the monotony around him and being so afraid and apprehensive that he knows that he could very easily start screaming. His stomach clenches and knots itself, and he mentally pictures all his inner organs breaking away from their fixed positions and moving around inside of him in a state of uproar. He concentrates on his breathing in an effort to calm his heart and relax his muscles.

He begins to wonder if the whole thing with the waiting room may be just a big joke or a bizarre way of testing his psychological endurance. He considers the possibility that he may eventually be channelled back to the front door of the building where he will be told that he is now free to return home. He holds on to the thought, willing it to be the truth but knowing that it most probably is not.

He remembers reading a book about a prisoner who after many years on Death Row was given a date for his execution. The day arrived, he ate a final meal of his own choosing, and was then led to the execution chamber. 'Dead man walking' was the term used to warn others as such a prisoner was moved from his cell to the chamber. This is how Arthur feels: *dead man walking*. He has been dead for a long time, he is sure of that now. Perhaps not dead in a physical sense but dead in all other senses. He may have died when he was moved into the flat on the third floor, or perhaps it was when he was told to forget his ambition to become a teacher and that he would instead be working at the Department of Discarded and Lost Property, or it may have been when his family had been disintegrated. In all probability, his death had been a collection of small deaths that had all led to where he is now.

Arthur tries to recall his parents' faces, but they are somewhat blurred, like old photos, and they lack important detail. Thinking about his parents makes him think, yet again, of his brother. Now when he is probably about to die he feels that it makes sense that he should be pulling his family around him, even if it is only in his thoughts. After he dies, no one will know; no one will be informed; no one will have any reason to mourn. There will be no gravestone, simply a small box carefully filed in the Department of Deceased Persons.

Arthur has visited the Department of Deceased Persons on only one occasion. A box of papers had arrived at the Department of Discarded and Lost Property, and after some investigation it was traced to a person who had died some three months earlier. Arthur's supervisor, not knowing what to do with the box, felt that the best thing to do was to deliver the box to the Department of Deceased Persons.

The Department of Deceased Persons was a sixty-storey building; as was the case in all sectors, it had been placed right at the centre of the collection of administrative buildings. It was the tallest of the ten or twelve buildings clustered together, and, like the other buildings, was known by its letter, which was the letter P.

Unlike the other buildings, it was not square or rectangular but was perfectly round. After climbing the fifty-four external steps to the front entrance and passing through the enormous revolving glass doors, Arthur had been awed by the magnificence of the foyer: the ceiling was high and the walls were a continuous, circular artwork in a swirling mixture of blue, green, and turquoise glass. At four points around the foyer there were information desks, and in the middle of the foyer was the lift. The walls of both the lift and the lift well itself were glass, which meant that one rose up through the building as an all-seeing being.

The woman at the closest information desk had sent Arthur and his box to the fourth floor where there were no coloured glass walls but plain white walls intercepted at well-spaced intervals by tall, thin windows. Arthur had stepped somewhat dizzily out of the lift and, after looking around the doughnut-shaped area, had made his way to the workspace that was directly in front of the lift.

A man in a dark blue uniform reverently took the box and placed it carefully on the polished-slate table behind him. There was nothing else on the table, and the box suddenly seemed to have been elevated to something that was well and truly beyond the ordinary description of a cardboard box.

Arthur stood for a moment, unsure of what to do next.

The man said: 'Perhaps you would like to see the resting place of 9411-220?'

Arthur was a little taken aback. As far as he knew, this was not part of his job description, but he was curious, so he nodded and said that he would.

They took the lift to the fifteenth floor. As they quietly and rapidly rose up through the centre of the building, Arthur was able to see how the resting floors were laid out, each one a complete replica of the one beneath. Like the walls on the fourth floor, there were tall windows letting in outside light, but in between all the windows, from floor to ceiling, the walls were honeycombed with hundreds, possibly thousands, of small rectangular openings. Some of these were already filled with brown boxes, and on the front of each small box there was a small silver plaque.

The man in the uniform politely motioned to Arthur to

step out of the lift before him while he checked a number on a small card. He then indicated that they should walk to the right, and there in front of them, about a third of the way up the wall, was the resting place of 9411-220. On the plaque there was simply the number 9411-220 and under the number there was a birth date and a date of death. Nothing more.

There were many spaces around 9411-220, and Arthur suddenly realized that resting places were allotted in numerical order: the spaces simply indicated that those people had not yet died.

A chill ran through his body, and he wondered where, and on which floor, was his space. Perhaps his parents were here, somewhere. He almost asked the man in the dark blue uniform, but then he remembered that his parents had had no numbers and, even if they had had numbers and even if Arthur had known what they were, it was unlikely that he would be given information pertaining to another sector. Also, the department for linking people from before the Change with the number system was in a separate building. Without a number the people at the Department of Deceased Persons would be unable to help him.

He wondered for a moment if it would be worth trying to find out his parents' numbers; at least he would then know whether they were living or dead, even if he did not know where they were.

His mind swung back to the immediate present. He was not quite sure what the etiquette was in such a place. Had it been a normal cemetery he would most probably have stood for a moment and, even if he had not prayed, would have thought about the person and wished him or her well. In a room with a lift well in the centre, even if the room was extremely large, and even if the sun was streaming in though the many window slits, everything felt strange, and well-wishes, and most definitely prayers, seemed weirdly out of place.

He hoped that the man had lived a happy life - a reasonably happy life at least. Arthur was no longer sure what real happiness was. He indicated to his companion that he was ready to leave, and the two men re-entered the lift.

Looking upwards, the man in the uniform spoke quietly. 'The crematorium is on the very top floor,' he said, 'but the smoke is taken care of before it leaves the building. Our clients leave no visible sign that they have passed from one dimension to another.'

Arthur found this sanitized approach to death somewhat abnormal, and it worried him that, eventually, this is where he would end up. This is where everyone in his sector ended up; even the man in the dark blue uniform would eventually end up here.

Arthur's guide left him at the fourth floor, and Arthur continued down to the ground floor. As he stepped out of the lift, he took a good look around the foyer, appreciating the artwork, enjoying the play of sunlight through the different colours, enjoying the architectural balance of the place. He knew that next time he was in the building he would not be in a state to be able to admire either the artwork or the design.

He does not want to return to the parking space and the little man, but his mind has a will of its own. He makes a compromise: if he must return, then he wants a reasonably happy outcome. He remembers the man talking about transfers, but he has not given any details, and Arthur is shying away from all the negative connotations of the word. He is trying to focus on something positive. If this is going to be his future, then he wants it to be long and anxiety-free.

He closes his eyes. He understands that he has now been living in a new Sector for several weeks. He is on the fifth floor of a grey and yellow tower block with an outlook over a wide blue-grey river lined with weeping willows. He is still working for the Department of Discarded and Lost Property, but now he is in Sector 36570, and everything is the same but different. The boy with the pimples is not there, but boxes are still being packed and taped and moved, and workers are still making lists on computing devices and cross-checking items against checklists of numbers and codes. Arthur still drinks coffee, in a different recreation room with different colleagues; no one asks questions and Arthur does not proffer any answers.

His experiences in the waiting room have made him realize just how anxious he has become, and he has been trying to do away with some of his routines and rituals. He has finally realized that instead of the routines removing his anxiety they have been tying him tighter and tighter to his many different neuroses, validating them and providing him with excuses to keep them alive. He has made a small amount of progress. Every day he makes himself do at least one thing differently, and although it is not always easy he is beginning to enjoy some of his small forays into slightly impulsive behaviour.

He does not always drink Earl Grey tea: he alternates with Darjeeling and English Breakfast. Some afternoons he walks along the riverside; other afternoons he works as a volunteer in the garden surrounding his tower block. He has joined a chess club, and although surveillance negates the possibility of his forming close friendships, he enjoys the mental stimulation.

When he was walking home from chess last Tuesday, he saw a man disappear into the tower block next to his.

The man, only slightly younger than himself, tall with fair hair and no glasses, reminded him of someone he once knew. He will keep his eyes open; perhaps he will see him again.

Arthur is still worrying about the girl and her bag, and his thoughts keep returning to the other girl - the girl he had ignored. He knows that he should have done something then, and perhaps this was his chance to make amends? Perhaps he should have spoken to the receptionist? Perhaps a compromise could be reached? There are so many instances of *perhaps* and no answers. While he tries to convince himself that, in the situation, he is doing the right thing by remaining quiet, everything else is niggling him, jostling for his attention. A feeling of disquiet begins to surge through his body, which only adds to the large clump of anxiety and stress that has been sitting there all afternoon. In fact, it has been there much longer; he can trace the beginning of its evolution to the day he found the letter in his letterbox.

He begins to move his weight on to his legs as a precursor to standing. He has decided that he *must* do something; he will try to talk to the receptionist; perhaps there is a slight chance that she will listen to reason, and if not—

'7891-447. To the door.'

Once again the sound is raucous and shrill, splitting the heavy silence in the room. He hesitates in his half-standing position. *He* is 7891-447. He lets his gaze move over all the people in the room, hoping against hope that there is another 7891-447, or that he misheard, or that the whole thing is a nightmare and that he will very soon wake up and be relieved that he is in his bed and not in a room full of plastic aqua-coloured chairs.

At the same time, he wonders if perhaps the decision to help the girl behind him has been made for him. Is it simply chance or are there other unknown forces at play? He does not know. He stands up and takes one last furtive look at the girl further along the row of chairs. This time their eyes connect for a brief second, and then he turns around and walks past all the chairs to the door in the middle of the front wall.

He is almost at the door, which he is sure will signal the end of everything. He fixes his eyes on the door - the door frame, the panels, the door handle - anxious to be able to remember exactly how everything looks before he is thrown into eternal blackness. He wonders if he will later have any memory of this instant.

Life is nothing more than a collection of *befores* and *afters*, he thinks. There is also something wedged between the before and the after, a sliver of *now*, but it is always overshadowed by the anticipation and the resolution. Arthur is not quite sure if *anticipation* and *resolution* are the correct words, but he knows what he means. He decides that the fact that he is about to be obliterated is of much greater significance, and discussion about the nuances or relevance of words is in actual fact not of any great importance.

He has often marvelled at the way seconds fall back into the *before* category almost simultaneously as he is anticipating them. He wonders: had the sum of his *befores* been different, could he have avoided his present *now*? He is quite sure that had he kept his head down and accepted the new regulations and not written letters and not been irritated by the new boy at work, he would not now be standing in a waiting room, facing a door that, once it closes behind him, will most certainly obliterate everything. His *now* could have been different and his anticipation not quite so terrifying.

Way back in his *then*, before the Change, he was studying to be a teacher. He had already completed two years of a three-year course, and he had no doubts about his career path. He could not wait for the time when he would be put in charge of his own class. All he wanted was to be able to hand on to children the same enthusiasm for learning and knowledge as he himself had experienced.

But he had not calculated with Unitas.

He is now standing in front of the door. He is not sure

any longer if it is natural wood, or white composite, or off-white fibreglass, or grey aluminium, or something else entirely different. He was certain that it was blonde oak but obviously things change, and his way of both seeing and relating to them also changes. He tries to pull his thoughts together into something that resembles logical thinking, and the more he looks at the door the more he decides that it *is* oak. But it is no longer the door itself that is important; it is what might be behind the door.

He cannot get the word *final* out of his head; he wonders what it will be like when there is a *before* and a *now* and no *then*. Will he have regrets for what he did not do, or will he regret all the wrong decisions he has made? Will he remember what it was like, standing in front of a door, worrying about the word *final*, or will everything be erased from his memory? The word *erase* soothes him a little. If that is the case, then there should be no anxiety, no pain, no regrets.

He has known all along that the letter was simply the beginning of something that was never meant to end happily for him. He has had several hours to analyse his situation, and he has come to the conclusion that he is going to be one of those people who simply disappear. He is not sure how he will disappear, but he knows that it will happen. He hopes that it will be painless - he has never been very brave when it comes to physical pain. If they intend to torture him, he will tell them everything, and much more as well, even as they are still sharpening their knives, checking their pliers, and adding fuel to the fire. He has no idea what they will be wanting to hear - perhaps something about his childhood or whether he likes his unit in the orange high-rise building. Or they may ask him about his conversation with the pimply youth. Yes, that is what they will ask him, and he will tell them everything. He will even tell them that he had woken late and missed breakfast, that he was in a very bad mood and that he did not like the boy. That he disliked the boy intensely.

And they will most probably look at each other and raise their eyebrows while they run their fingers along sharpened blades or test the weight of heavy mallets, uninterested in what he has to say and totally focused on what they are about to do.

Or perhaps there will be no questions, no interrogation, no torture, simply a couple of officials, a lift to the basement, a waiting ambulance, a gurney. Arthur does not want to follow this train of thought; it is bounding ahead of him in a direction he does not want to follow, not even in his mind.

He forces his thoughts back to the possibility that his imagination is creating outlandish scenarios that most probably are not true. Beyond that door there will be a dental surgery or a tax worker. He holds that thought in the front of his mind; he wants to believe that it is the truth and he wonders if, by believing in it, he can make it real.

He places his hand on the door and hesitates for a moment. He thinks of how it was before the Change, when terminally ill people who wanted to end their lives would book themselves into a euthanasia clinic. There they would eventually be hooked up to the machine that would hopefully bring them the relief they were seeking. Lying on the bed, the cannula in their arm, the poisoned liquid ready to flow down the tubing and into their blood stream, they would have been very much in the *before*, knowing that the *now* and the *then* were completely up to them. No one else would push the button that would set the liquid flowing through the tubing; this was their own decision, their own life and their own death.

He knows that he has no other option than to open the door leading from the waiting room and then to step across the threshold, and he knows without a doubt that he is taking his life into his own hands. It is not a choice he is making freely: he might well be the one opening the door, but the receptionist would scarcely have considered the other option, that is of allowing him *not* to open the door. He wonders if the way he is feeling is somehow the same as being chased by a horde of man-eating dogs along a narrow tunnel towards a three-hundred metre cliff drop. Whether he hurls himself over the cliff or opens the door, the decision to do so has already been carefully planned by others intent on his destruction.

Will there be a clean, sunlit doctor's surgery waiting for him on the other side of the door; or will the door open out above a void into which he will fall, his arms and legs flailing helplessly as the darkness closes over him; or will there be a corridor and tubes of high-powered lighting and arrows funnelling him towards a room where serious-faced judges will don black caps before passing sentence?

There is no way he can know.

Arthur hesitates a little longer and then, closing his eyes, he opens the door.

The door closes behind him with a soft click.

THEA

Thea is extremely aware that she is running late, and although she wishes she could turn back time an hour, or even half an hour, she is resigned to not getting her wish. The letter had specified six o'clock (or, to be correct, 18.00), but she had left home much later than she had intended and had not given any thought to the fact that it was peak hour. Then, when she finally stepped off the bus outside the cluster of administrative buildings, she spent ages trying to find the entrance to Building C: there were three different entrances, each of them servicing only a specific block of floors. Once inside the correct part of the building, she had run around in circles, looking for her lift in a complicated jungle of lifts, all of them with a different stopping pattern.

She has a bad habit of running late: more than

anything she hates arriving early and then having to wait around, doing nothing, and as a result she often arrives late.

Having finally found the correct lift for floor thirty-six, she swipes her PB across the stainless-steel control panel and marvels at how quietly and quickly she reaches her destination. She catches her breath as she steps out of the lift, realizing that she has been moved thirty-six floors above where she was standing only seconds ago. She does a quick mental calculation and guesses that she must be about one hundred and fifty metres above the ground. The thought is sobering, but she has still not collected herself after all the rushing and stress, and she now hurries breathlessly along the corridor, her almost new, soft-soled shoes making a smooth smacking sound on the timber flooring. There is no one else to be seen in the corridor, and she begins to worry as to whether or not she is on the right floor. If she had not been in such a dreadful hurry, and if she had not been so stressed, she would have double-checked the floor number when she got out of the lift. She assumes that it is floor thirty-six, but she had expected to see other people, and she finds the long, empty corridor both intimidating and a cause for concern.

By the time she reaches the door at the end of the corridor she is even more out of breath - a combination of physical activity and mental anguish. She notes the clean, black-on-white label *Waiting Room* in the middle of the door, before standing perfectly still for a moment, with her eyes closed, trying to pull herself into something that resembles normality. Then she opens her eyes, straightens her coat, adjusts her bag, and, pushing gently against the door, steps inside the room.

The waiting room is much larger than she had expected. It is rectangular in shape, with the door on one of the long sides. She does not manage to assimilate much more than the size and the shape of the room before she sees the receptionist at her desk.

Within the space of only a few seconds, Thea has summed up the receptionist, and she is more than certain that such an unsympathetic-looking woman would not be the least bit interested in hearing how time can get compressed and that the building has a confusing lift system. Also, quite certain that there is absolutely no point in trying to explain her lateness, she places the letter on the desk without saying a word. From her fairly limited experience, medical appointments never seem to keep to the schedule, so though she is stressed about being late she does not expect that the delay will have disturbed the general routine overly much.

As the receptionist does not look up or even acknowledge that Thea is standing in front of her, Thea begins to wonder if perhaps she has been rendered completely invisible, and she watches with some degree of confusion as the woman carefully finishes the row she is working on and then places her knitting demonstratively on the desk. At this point, Thea is more than a little taken aback as the receptionist sighs audibly and, for the first time, looks directly at her.

Obviously she is not invisible at all.

The receptionist then picks up the letter from the desk, reprimands Thea for arriving twenty minutes past the stipulated time, and, without even drawing a breath, points demonstratively at the large patchwork bag slung over Thea's shoulder.

'No personal effects,' she says.

'But it's my *bag*.' Thea retorts, holding the strap hard in her hand. 'I don't go anywhere without it.'

The receptionist glares at Thea; she clearly has no intention of letting her keep her bag, and, leaning across the desk, she grabs hold of the strap.

In spite of her somewhat anorexic appearance, the woman is extremely strong and her grip is unflinching. Thea does not want the bag destroyed, so she finally relinquishes her hold and watches while the woman, somewhat triumphantly, places it on her desk.

'I'll get it back, won't I? Afterwards?' Thea asks.

The woman says nothing, writes Thea's number on a piece of paper, places the paper on the smaller of the two piles in front of her and points impatiently to the chairs in the middle of the room.

Thea sits down on an empty chair in the back row, wondering vaguely if it has been recently vacated or whether it has been empty all the time. Her mind backtracks a little as she realizes that the waiting room must have been open all day, and it is hardly likely that the chair has been vacant for so many hours on end.

She undoes the top three buttons of her coat - it is much warmer in the waiting room than she was expecting - and then takes a quick look at the other people in the room. There is a man at the end of the row who seems to be somewhat sympathetic; he actually glances in her direction and smiles encouragingly. Thea cannot think of anything to smile about - she is still concerned about her bag - but she appreciates the gesture. She feels bad about not smiling back, but she cannot do anything about it, and she just hopes that he understands.

Looking around the room, or as much of it as she can see from where she is sitting, she notes the pale yellow walls, the dark grey door at the front of the room and, when she turns her head to the left, the steel table with the charcoal-coloured glass top where her bag is now resting in full view. As much as she can see of the receptionist's chair, she guesses that it is also charcoal grey and padded, which is something her chair is not. Thea takes a fleeting look at the receptionist and wonders if she has been just as difficult with everyone else in the room. She makes a mental note to speak to someone about the woman's extremely rude behaviour; she expects that she will be able to see someone in authority once she leaves the waiting room.

She is slightly surprised that the encounter with the receptionist has upset her so much, but she has never coped very well with aggressive people. Close to tears, she is doing her best not to start crying, especially not over something that is so stupid and so unfair. While she is unable to keep her hands from trembling, her whole body has become tense, and her heart is beating faster than normal. On top of all the worry at being late she is now even more agitated because of the unpleasant woman.

She cannot remember having been treated so rudely before. She accepts that she has arrived later than she should have, but it is a simple medical appointment - it is not as though it is a State function where she is the guest of honour. Sometimes things do not go completely to plan, and sometimes it is difficult to keep to a timetable, yet she is being treated as though she is some kind of deranged person or criminal, needing to be severely disciplined. She is both irritated and angry, but does not feel that she is in a position where she can say what she thinks. In any other situation, she would most probably have told the woman exactly what she thought of her, or, at the very least, would have demanded to speak with her supervisor or even walked out of the room, but something tells her that none of these responses would have been a particularly good idea. So she sits on her hands and seethes and thinks about her bag, a vital part of herself, lying only a few metres behind her.

She tries to remember all the things she has in the bag, private things, things that are an important part of who she is, but before she has finished making a mental list, her thoughts dart off in another direction and collect themselves around the very little she knows about the man sitting further across to her right. The man who smiled at her.

From that one hasty look, she has calculated that he is possibly in his mid- to late thirties. He seems taller than average - though it is not always easy to judge when someone is sitting down - well-dressed, and, more import- antly, probably sympathetic. Or empathetic? Thea halts briefly in her train of thought and wonders which of the two words is more correct. If it were possible to talk to the man, acknowledge his look that seemed supportive and his possible understanding of her situation, she would do so. The more she thinks about the man, the more she believes that he is the type of person who is aware of others, a positive trait that is unquestionably on the wane. Everyone sees things differently, but whatever they see and however they look at what they see, Thea feels that they should always do it through a filter of empathy or sympathy; surely that would be a step towards making the world a better, happier place?

Normally she does not dwell too much on things like happiness and the state of the world: life, as far as she is concerned, is quite satisfactory. She is aware that for some people - like herself, for example - it is probably more satisfactory than for many others, but she is an optimist and cannot see any point in focusing on unlikely negatives.

She moves a little on her chair and shakes her head, sending the thoughts about sympathy and awareness in different directions. She is most probably reading far too much into a hasty glance. Perhaps he has hardly seen her, because in all likelihood all his concentration is elsewhere.

Her heart rate is slowly returning to normal as she makes a concerted effort to move her thoughts away from the ill-disposed receptionist and even from the man seated a few chairs from her on her right. She notices that there are already a number of empty chairs in both rows, and she is hoping that it is a sign that she will not have to wait very long. Thinking about waiting moves her thoughts back to her bag on the receptionist's desk, and she begins to feel upset and angry again, so she consciously forces herself to think of everything she would rather be doing instead of sitting in a waiting room with the worst receptionist she has ever had the misfortune of meeting.

While Thea is worrying about her bag, trying not to think about unfriendly receptionists, and wondering whether the man a few seats away is sympathetic or empathetic or something else entirely, and before she is able to fully steer her thoughts in the direction of other, less confronting, things, the receptionist suddenly calls out: '7891-447. To the door.'

Thea is uncomfortably jolted out of her thoughts, believing for a split second that perhaps *she* is 7891-447, before realizing that she is not. She looks around, vaguely interested to see who owns the number, and sees that it belongs to the man with the smile.

He is already standing up, but before he starts to move towards the door he looks across at Thea a second time. This time he is not smiling, though his look is still kind, even compassionate. Had the circumstances been different: had they been sitting closer or had the receptionist been normally pleasant, Thea is certain that she would have said something to him. He seems serious, possibly anxious, and Thea wonders if he suspects that he has some terminal illness. Perhaps he already knows that he has months, perhaps only weeks, to live.

She watches him as he walks slowly towards the door and then disappears.

The incident with the man has upset her more than she would like to admit. She finds it strange: after all, she did not even know the man; the only contact they had had was the smile he sent in her direction. She appreciated both his smile and the feeling that he understood her situation and that he most probably would have even sided with her against the impossible receptionist, but there is a possibility that she may have got it all wrong. The thought that she may have misunderstood both the man and his smile swells and fills her mind before she quickly discards it; she is usually right about people, and she knows that the man who just disappeared through the door was sympathetic and kind.

She empties her mind, closing her eyes while sending the man some positive, healing thoughts. By the time she has reopened her eyes some seconds later, she has cleared her mind of the man, his smile, and his imminent death, and has focused her thoughts on how she had phoned the Department of Health and Wellness only a week ago and asked for an appointment.

She has been having considerable pain in her right shoulder. She has had it for a long time - several months at least - but lately it has got much worse, and sometimes it keeps her awake all night. When she mentioned it to her supervisor, she was immediately taken off the wheel and put in the glaze room, but Thea knows that if it does not get better and if the supervisor feels that her work is slipping, she will be reassigned. There will be a meeting at the Department of Work and Occupation, and she will be allocated new employment in a completely different area. The realization that she might be moved from the Ceramics Factory has shaken Thea, and she has been trying to keep to a strict routine of applying heat creams and taking pain relief. She really hopes that the shoulder will eventually right itself, but one of the girls she works with has been nagging her to have it looked at professionally. 'It could be something else,' she said, 'something really bad.'

Thea does not believe that the pain in her shoulder is something that is *really bad,* but she contacted the Department anyway, and the secretary took her details and said that she would receive a letter with information about an appointment date and time. In the meantime, Thea did her own research and decided that it is probably something that could be fixed with a cortisone injection - at least, that is what she is hoping; she is having difficulty getting the words *really bad* out of her head. Perhaps it is early onset arthritis, or, even worse, perhaps it is a tumour.

Then, a day or so later, while she was tossing all these possibilities around in her head, she received a letter that admittedly did not mention the Department of Health and Wellness but which told her to present herself at Building C. The vagueness of the letter concerned her a little at first, but she is still almost certain that she has been called to the building for her medical appointment: it could not possibly be anything else. She cannot understand why this was not stated in the letter itself; it would have made everything more transparent and less stressful. That there was no letterhead from the Department of Health and Wellness has been hanging there like a grey shadow at the back of her mind: should she be concerned, or should she simply accept it as one of those small errors that can creep into any department no matter how efficiently it is normally run? She does not particularly like medical appointments at the best of times, but, if she is honest with herself, the letter has made the whole thing so much more disturbing. She is trying to remember where she went the last time she had to see a doctor; she is certain that it was Building C, but she can no longer remember which floor.

The letter had specified that she was to arrive at six in the evening, but by the time she had got home from work it was later than usual, and she had barely had time to eat dinner before a girlfriend contacted her on her PS, and, finally, when she realized how late it was she also realized that she had miscalculated how long it would take to reach the building. When she arrived at Building C she was already at least ten minutes late, and she had then spent a further ten minutes looking for the right lift.

Perhaps it was those twenty minutes past the stated time that had caused the receptionist to collapse into hysteria, or perhaps the woman would have been hysterical no matter when Thea had walked through the door and whether she had had her bag with her or not.

Thea sighs yet again and moves her hands into her lap. She looks at all the people sitting in the room, doing nothing, saying nothing; then she belatedly remembers the bit about not being allowed to have any personal possessions. It was such a strange request, and she remembers, when she received the letter, how she wondered why it was so important, before she finally discarded it as a printing error and not something that concerned her. Then, thinking how thin the line is between something being believable and unbelievable, her mind wanders back to her bag sitting on the reception desk and, eventually, back to what she might have been doing had she not been called to Building C.

When she spoke with the woman at the Department of Health and Wellness, she had insisted on a late appointment, so when she read that she was to be at Building C at 18.00 she had been relieved that someone had been listening to her. She is thinking of this now, and she comes to the conclusion that the time of the appointment must prove that floor thirty-six is the home of Health and Wellness and that consulting rooms, and nothing else, are on the other side of the waiting room door; no one else knew that she needed a late appointment. While she tries to work up a small amount of enthusiasm at her discovery, she cannot move her thoughts from the letter without a letterhead and the very unpleasant receptionist.

She is also thinking about the conversation she had with her girlfriend, although what degree of friendship is denoted by the term *friend* is something about which Thea is not completely sure. Given the restrictions on forming close friendships, the concepts *friend* and *close friend* have been reassessed: a friend, according to Unitas, is the person you work with, the person who lives next door, the person you happen to meet in the park or at the purchase centre. As far as Unitas is concerned, everyone is part of a big happy family, all working for the good of the whole; it is not only expected but required that everyone be friends with everyone else. On the other hand, exclusive, close friendships, especially among children, are frowned upon, even banned; the idea of 'best friends' is anathema to Unitas. Having grown up as part of a group held together by a web of superficial friendships, Thea is not complete-ly sure where the line goes between such ordinary, approved friendships and friendships that are closer and more important. She is not even sure if there is a line, everything having been made as homogeneous as possible.

3030-772, nicknamed Jule, had appeared on her PS just as Thea was cleaning up after a very hurried meal. Nicknames are discouraged, but people use them anyway: having to use a seven- or eight-digit number every time one needs to refer to someone can become both tedious and frustrating. But nicknames are used with care and never around anyone in authority.

Jule had been extremely upset, and Thea, who had had one eye following the minute hand on the clock, during the entire time they were talking, now feels that she did not give her the emotional support she was looking for. Jule's daughter, who was about to turn three, was to be taken from her and placed in one of the many homes for small children in a completely different sector. This was not at all unexpected - in fact, it was normal procedure - but the awful reality of it had not been rammed home until Jule received a letter from the Department of Childhood Advancement and Protection, usually abbreviated to DCAP, reminding her that her daughter would be collected on the twenty-ninth day of that month at nine in the morning. Her birthday.

Thea would never admit that she has given any thought to the practice of removing children from their parents, but she knows that, occasionally, she does wonder about the relationship between a child and its mother, and if it is something that is important. She does not want to feel that Unitas is wrong in sundering this relationship, but there have been times when she has felt a sudden emptiness, or perhaps it could be described as a longing after something for which she has no name. She wonders briefly if children should, perhaps, remain with their mothers, and then the thought passes, and she tells herself that Unitas knows best.

Thea, like the rest of her generation, grew up in State-run institutions where she believes that she had a happy childhood: she was well looked after, she did not want for anything, so obviously the system worked. She is not quite sure what would happen if Jule were to keep her daughter. Thea doubts that she would be able to give her the same kind of satisfactory, all-round upbringing that Unitas could give her. Deciding that such an idea - that anyone should bring up their own child - is impossible, she wonders what would eventually happen to such children: they would probably become social outcasts. But, as she listens to Jule, a large question mark appears at the back of her mind: what if Jule is right and Unitas is wrong? She concentrates on pushing the thought to one side: Unitas cannot be wrong.

Then she remembers the emptiness, and she is no longer completely sure.

'She's my daughter!' Jule had wept on the other side of the screen, while Thea watched the clock and thought about emptiness and whether there was a chance that Unitas had got it all wrong. Now, when Thea thinks back on the conversation, she pushes aside her ideas of what constitutes a satisfactory upbringing and is shaken by a feeling of déjà vu. She wonders what bit the system does not like, and she asks herself if it could be the *my* bit - my child, my parents, my house, my bag. The idea of *my* is not part of the system; it was replaced years ago with the more inclusive *our*.

When it came to the physical aspects of the society in which she lived, Thea knew that her life to date did not include many other memories than those of the orange, yellow, and grey tower blocks that were encroaching more and more on the smaller dwellings of the sector, with the very much taller administrative buildings at its centre. All other memories related to the words *home* and *place* were so vague that she was not really aware that life could be any different to what she was used to. She had no concept of the original meaning of the word *family*; now it was only used to refer to groups within Unitas. Unitas itself was often referred to as the ultimate family group, but within this all-embracing family there were many smaller families, all of them with some political connection, and all of them part of Unitas.

She did have a family, once; though the images and the descriptions were diffuse and scattered. She could remember being very small, living in a house with dark passageways and high, white ceilings. She could remember a man's long grey trouser legs and some red platform shoes that must have belonged to her mother. When the snippets of scattered information came together, she learnt that her father was a saxophone player with the city orchestra and her mother was a painter. When she first heard that her mother was a painter she had thought of ceilings and walls, but the person who was attempting to bring the scattered information together then added that her mother painted pictures. 'Portraits, mainly,' she had explained, 'but even abstracts.'

Thea had been delighted to hear about her artistic parents, but, for her, they were little more than interesting strangers. She had lived with them in the house with the high ceilings until she was six years old when she was sent away.

This seismic alteration to her life path occurred shortly after the Change came into full effect. The new government had looked at childcare and before- and after-school care and vacation care and decided that the system of caring for children needed to be revolutionized. Behind the locked doors of their meeting rooms, different government ministers and officials argued that as children spent the greater part of the day being cared for by people other than their parents it made sense to streamline the entire system. From the age of three, children would be moved to state-run institutions where they would be cared for, educated, and immersed in the policies and ideals of the new regime. They acknowledged that there would have to be a transition period where the first intakes would be comprised of children up to the age of fifteen. Fully aware that the first participants of the scheme would have spent their growing-up years in a very different system to the one they were proposing, they advocated that the staff at these institutions should not only put an emphasis on ideals and the basic concepts behind Unitas but should also treat the children with special kindness and understanding.

As a six-year-old, Thea was moved to a home with other six-year-olds. Although she may have initially missed her parents, her new life gradually elbowed out her earlier memories and images until, at last, she was left with not much more than the long, grey trouser legs and the red platform shoes. As far as she was concerned, the Children's Home was home, and she found it difficult to imagine that life could be otherwise. Many ideas and concepts from her very early childhood had been either erased or completely changed. People never spoke about the past; it was as though it had never existed. She had no reason to wonder why life was the way it was, because, as far as she knew, that is the way it had always been.

In the same way that generations before her had felt that the idea of towns, villages, and even cities was completely normal, she believed, even as she grew older, that the concept of sectors was unremarkable. By the time she was in her teens, she knew that the entire country was divided up into areas called sectors, all of them very much like the one where she lived, and she could accept that movement around the country had to be monitored and supervised. Permission to travel to another sector was based on an application being lodged through the correct channels, and all the paperwork being approved. Most people found the process too complicated and opted to stay where they were; others, mainly department officials or those who needed to travel because of work, were usually on top of the application process and simply looked on it as one of those irritating inconveniences that could not be avoided. Middle-management and senior

155

officials were issued with border-free passes four times a year.

Beyond the houses and the tower blocks in any sector there was a wide recreational area that more or less circled the entire sector; beyond the recreational area, with its trees and walkways and expanses of grass, Thea had heard rumours that there was some kind of invisible intrusion-detection system to keep the people who lived in that particular sector in and others out. She was not sure if she believed what she had heard, but she did not find the possibility at all threatening: it was simply part of the overall security system.

She had never been further than the recreational band, but on those occasions she had been there she had looked across the open ground and wondered about the invisible fence. Because it was impossible to leave the area without the specific permit having been programmed into her PB, she did not spend too much time thinking about life beyond her sector. Thea remembers being told how, many, many years ago, people used to travel everywhere in their own vehicles, but practically no one owned cars now. Even before Unitas came to power, all old cars had been forcibly de-registered and removed, though these so-called *old* electric and solar cars were in fact not that old, having only replaced the petrol and diesel ones more than two decades earlier. During the first two years after the Change, Administration managed to remove almost all cars. No one knew where the cars went: some said that they were used for landfill; others were certain that they were recycled; still others believed that they had been sold to another country or else dumped in the ocean. The very few cars that remained were subjected to a whole list of restrictions. Though many people felt that there was little point in owning a car when permission had to be sought simply to move between sectors, there were some who treasured the small sliver of personal freedom a car gave them. A few of the higher officials still drove cars, but most of them now had access to hovers.

Transport had been communal for as long as Thea could remember. Driverless buses covered the entire sector and ran efficiently around the clock. Between the sectors there was a spiderweb of fast automatic trains; people could no longer understand why anyone would need or want a vehicle of their own.

Thea's first real memories, excluding cars, dark hallways, high ceilings, grey trouser legs and red shoes, are from the home for little children, and these memories involve lots of other children of her own age dressed in brown overalls. Somewhere on the edges of these memories there are tall people who seem to be all shadows, dark blue skirts and legs – legs now covered in dark blue instead of grey. Then, when she turned ten, she was moved to a second home, which was for older children, and here she spent the next five years.

As Thea's new memories took shape during her time in the Children's Homes, her few old memories remained tucked well away in the back of her mind. During the first couple of years, children were not allowed to have any contact with their parents, as it was argued that this would make the change from parental home to state institution too difficult, if not traumatic, for both the child and its parents. After the initial two years, Thea remembered being brought to a special visitors' room in the Home to meet her parents. She was not too sure what the word *parents* implied, but other children who had already met their parents, and whose understanding of the word was just as vague as Thea's, told her that they were the people she had lived with before she came to the Home.

When she arrived in the sunlit, but very sterile-looking, visitors' room, there were two people sitting together on a chunky blue sofa. There was a table in front of them, and on the other side of the table another identical blue sofa. The blonde timber of the floor was repeated in the window frames and the small table. On the walls behind the two sofas, there were almost identical paintings of white gladioli in dark blue vases. There was nothing else in the room.

If Thea was subconsciously clinging to her memories of red shoes and grey trousers, there was nothing about the two people in front of her that connected them to such memories. The man was dressed in black trousers with a collarless white shirt; the woman had a deep purple skirt, black jumper, and black low-heeled shoes. She shook hands almost self-consciously with the two people and then sat down on the edge of the sofa opposite them. The matron who had accompanied her to the room remained standing near the door, physically apart from the trio on the sofas but mentally and emotionally filling the entire room.

The parents had been warned in advance that there was to be no familiar touching, indeed nothing that might cause an emotional scene. They had been told that it was for the child's best, that there was no point in upsetting the child for a half-hour visit.

Half an hour.

Later, when Thea was older, she decided that half an hour twice a year was probably a little on the miserly side; however, she could not say that it had a negative effect on her. The people who were introduced to her as parents were pleasant enough, but she did not know them, and one hour a year was hardly going to change things. She remembered that first time when they visited: she was eight or nine. Everyone was so very polite and the conversation so very stilted that she was glad when the matron called out that the visit had come to an end and they could say goodbye.

As she became older, the visits did not change: What kind of things do you do here in the Children's Home?

What are you learning at school? Do you have a best friend? (At which point the matron, or whoever it was standing near the door, interrupted saying, 'We don't have best friends; we are friends with everyone.'). Eventually, Thea learnt about the saxophone and the paintings, but this was several years after the visits had petered out. She thought of all the things she would have liked to have asked the two people who were her parents, but it was too late. No doubt the strain of the limited, non-emotional visits was too much for them; finally accepting the hard-to-accept fact that they would never again be able to relate to Thea as their child, they stopped visiting. The ordeal of sitting so close to her, while being confined within a set of draconian regulations, only exacerbated their sense of loss.

They did occasionally write letters - and the fact that the letters were non-digital told Thea that they would have to have come through official channels (only official, non-digital letters were given access to private letterboxes) – but, whether it was due to redacting or to an unwillingness on her parents' part to overstep the boundary that had been set in place by Unitas, the letters never told her anything more than the uncomfortable visits in the visitors' room. Once she turned fifteen, the letters stopped completely.

By the time she had turned fifteen, the memories of the red shoes and the grey trousers had been slightly filled out by the few times she had been permitted to see her parents. She felt that it was nice to have the memories, however abbreviated, but she told herself that she did not miss what she had never really experienced, and, instead, looked forward to the next stage of her life.

After a number of interviews and psychological assessments, she was selected for a training centre where she was taught how to turn clay into practical everyday objects. She enjoyed working with the white-grey material, which in many ways was almost living and often had a will of its own. The cups and bowls and vases that she fashioned were like small individuals, each of them unique, and each of them possessing just a very small part of her, their creator.

After two years at the training centre, she graduated to a ceramics factory where she rotated between the wheel, the glazing and decorating rooms, and the kiln room. When she received the letter, telling her to come to floor thirty-six, she had already been at the factory for five years - she was now twenty-two - and although she had no experience of any other kind of life, she loved her work. Not having anything with which to compare her situation, she had fully believed that she was happy. And then, six months before receiving her letter, she met Aaron.

She rubs her shoulder carefully. Without question the pain has got much worse, but, then again, she has been extremely stressed, and she has heard that stress can cause a whole litany of problems. She rummages in one of her coat pockets for a small blister pack of pain tablets, and pops out a white pain tablet without removing the pack from her pocket. She reflects on how lucky she was to have moved the tablets to her pocket while she was still in the lift; they could so easily have been sitting in her bag on the receptionist's desk. Still holding the tablet between her fingers, she glances around, wondering if she might be able to get some water somewhere. Most medical waiting rooms have a water dispenser and paper cups, but from what she has so far seen of the waiting room, she is not at all optimistic about there being a water dispenser of any shape or form, and she really does not want to approach the receptionist. She places the tablet in her mouth and hopes that her saliva will be sufficient to wash it down. As she bites down on the tablet, a bitter taste fills her mouth, and she thinks of all the reasons tablets should be taken with water. She is wondering if she will later look back with the sudden realization that this was when her stomach or throat problem began.

The bitter taste begins slowly to subside and she looks forward to getting some respite from her pain. Thinking about respite makes her more aware of the pain itself. She is quite sure that the pain is work-related, but since someone had suggested that it could be something else, the thought has remained, niggling in the back of her head. Perhaps it *is* something else, and perhaps that something *is* really bad.

Thea tries to move on from such thoughts; she consoles herself with the thought that she is in the right place to get assistance, and she commends herself that she actually went ahead and made the appointment.

Her mind will not let go of her bag that is still sitting on the receptionist's desk. The image of the bag and its contents keeps pulling her awareness back to the steel and glass desk at the back of the room. She feels strangely naked without it; were it at all possible she would have turned around and grabbed it back, but it is not possible, and she moves her attention to her hands, now resting on her lap. She knows that she will soon be able to talk to someone in charge, and the thought calms her a little.

She made the bag herself from a pile of material remnants she found in her sewing box. There was emerald green left over from a skirt she had sewn a couple of years ago; a piece of blue and purple patterned cotton;

some scarlet fabric; several pieces of cloth with an abstract pattern in a number of different colours; a square of sunflower-yellow corduroy; some red-checked material from a discarded tablecloth. She had hand-sewn the little squares meticulously, placing them together in a pattern that was more dictated by her mood than aesthetics. Each small square of colour meant something different to her, reminding her of things she had done, people she had met, and thoughts she entertained, if only briefly.

Looking out over the other people in the room, she is hoping that her number will be the next one called. She turns and looks at the clock on the wall behind her - her PS, of course, is in her bag - and calculates how long she has been in the waiting room. She cannot remember having to wait so long on her previous visit to the medical centre, but that was at least two or three years ago, and it is possible that things have changed since then.

Her thoughts move away from clocks and time and medical appointments and push their way towards Aaron, but her mood changes before they reach him, and they veer off again and wrap around the man who had been sitting in the waiting room. She wonders where he is now, and whether everything went all right for him with his appointment: she wonders if he is still somewhere in the Health Centre. She is hoping that she may be able to meet him later and thank him. She is not sure what she wants to thank him for, but he did seem understanding and sympathetic.

She pushes thoughts about the man from the waiting room to one side, and she tries to remember what the medical centre looked like when she was there last. From what she remembers, the waiting room was completely different, so perhaps they have a number of centres on different floors. The centre she last visited was a large, airy functional space with rows of doors on each side. She is no longer sure of the colour scheme: it could have been yellow and grey, but then again, perhaps she is being influenced by the colour scheme in the present waiting room, and perhaps it was something entirely different. She is almost certain that there was a circular area in the centre of the space with a continuous charcoal-coloured glass counter and transparent glass walls in narrow strips, allowing clients access to both the counter and the couple of uniform-clad women on the other side. Her thoughts hesitate at this point, questioning whether the counter was charcoal-grey or whether it was blue or green or even the colour of natural timber.

The tablet has finally begun to take the edge off her pain, and she is again thinking about the man who had looked at her, remembering that although the look was brief he seemed compassionate. She likes to think that he most possibly agreed with her about the bag and that he felt the way she had been treated was unwarranted. Although she has no way of really knowing, she believes that he may have wanted to help her.

At seven forty-five another man is called to the door, and Thea turns around and looks impatiently at the clock on the wall. She would have expected her number to have been called before now even though she arrived late. Thea has always been impulsive and impatient: if she decides to do something, she does it without delay, and she expects others to act in a similar fashion. Waiting rooms may be necessary in places like medical clinics, but as far as Thea is concerned, the waiting bit should be kept to a minimum.

She turns in her chair and looks questioningly at the receptionist, but the woman ignores her and continues with whatever it is that is requiring her attention on her PS. For a moment, Thea wonders, somewhat irrationally, whether the woman is simply holding her back in order to spite her. She has decided that she does not like the woman - a feeling that is greatly emphasized by the fact that the time schedule seems to be all over the place. Then she wonders if there may have been an emergency earlier in the afternoon before she arrived. If that is the case, then perhaps everyone in the waiting room is running late, and perhaps everyone is just as irritated as she is. If an emergency has impacted on the schedule, then she can hardly blame the late-running appointments on the receptionist.

Aaron, or 7651-227, is tall and fair-haired with grey-blue eyes and a three-day beard. He works in administration at the ceramics factory and is almost ten years older than Thea; while she remembers very little of life before the Change, he still has a vivid recollection of his early years in a normal family environment with parents and three siblings. Although he has been issued with a number - 7651-227 - and a number badge, which he is obliged to wear at all times, he has not forgotten his name, and when he thinks of himself it is always as Aaron and never as 7651-227. When he first met Thea at the factory, he had introduced himself as Aaron before he quickly corrected himself.

But Thea's interest was aroused. She knew that people used to have 'names', but she had never met anyone using a real name, not just a nickname. Nowadays, people normally pointed to their badges when they introduced themselves, but Thea had heard that, long ago, the complicated number combinations were even used in conversation. She turned the name *Aaron* around between her lips, savouring the vowels, lingering over the two syllables, loving the way it all sounded.

After he corrected himself he had said quietly: 'You would most probably also have had a name, once, a long time ago.'

Thea, who has only ever known herself as 3325-678, was excited to think that she, too, might be the owner of a collection of sounds that could move elegantly around the mouth and rest softly on the lips. Admittedly, she had always suspected that she had had a name, but both of the Children's Homes had done a very good job of wiping it from her memory. Her number identifies her, but it is not really part of her; it is not her name; it does not capture the essence of who she is in the way that her real name would have to capture everything about her.

He, in turn, was fascinated by the girl with the long brown hair, and he promised her that he would try to find out what her name had been before, before things changed. His work allows him easy access to most of the information connected to the factory, so while giving the impression that he is cross-checking production numbers and employee schedules, he accesses the file for 3325-678. His eyes quickly scan the first two or three lines of information that flash across the screen as the file opens. The most important piece of information, though, is the name: 3325-678 - Thea Robinson.

The ceramics factory is fairly close to the edge of the sector, close to the river. It is an old, rambling red-brick building that has been there since well before the Change. It is one of a few structures that have been allowed to stand while others in the town have been razed and rebuilt. Over the years since the Change, parts of the factory have been renovated, and smaller, work-specific buildings have been added. For those who still have any memory of life before the Change, the red-brick ceramics building symbolizes all those things that have been irrevocably swept away.

It stands at the top of a rise that climbs very gradually from the road and then falls away towards the river at the back of the building. Sprawling and much wider than it is deep, the ceramics building with its tiled roofs, green-grey doors and, at one side, the partially covered kiln area radiates a sense of stability and authority.

No one lives on the property, everyone commuting daily on the 603 bus from an orange or grey or white tower block near the centre of the sector or from one of the single dwellings that have managed to evade destruction. The ceramics factory is the end of the line for the driverless, bio-fuelled 603, after which the bus follows the loop around the green terminal shed and then heads back to the centre.

Thea had very occasionally seen Aaron on the bus, though she had no idea who he was or that his *name* was Aaron. She has practically nothing to do with anyone from ceramics administration; the administration building is one of the purpose-built buildings in the grounds of the factory itself, closer to the entrance to the property than to the factory itself. She possibly would never have had met Aaron had he not had occasion to come down to the factory one day, about six months ago. He needed to check numbers of a certain mug design that had only been in production for a couple of months. It was while he had been speaking with the supervisor that he had looked across the room and, for no specific reason, locked glances with Thea, who just then lifted her eyes from the wheel.

After that first visit, Aaron often had cause to check production figures at the factory, and he learnt to time his visits so that he could spend a few minutes with Thea when she was on her break. They would always meet as though by accident, and they usually kept to the paved courtyard area at the back of the building. The large flat red stones were nestled between two long, out-jutting walls - one belonging to the throwing room, the other a storeroom - both without windows. The small area thus formed was a hidden place where a worker could grab a few solitary moments, enjoying the feeling of warm sun on his or her face and perhaps relishing the image and the sounds of the river only metres away. It was on the first of these breaks that Aaron had introduced himself and then added: 'You would have also had a name, once, a long time ago.'

And the following week he told her that her name was Thea.

Thea cannot help thinking about Jule. She attempts to put herself into Jule's situation, imagining that she has a child and that that child is about to be taken away. She concentrates on summoning up images of the woman with the red platform shoes - her mother - and she wonders if she felt the same as Jule when *her* child was taken away. The thought troubles her a little: she has never given much thought to how her mother must have felt; images of the stilted half-hour meetings fill her mind, making her reflect, yet again, on emptiness and longing.

She has never had a deep emotional connection with anyone, though she must have connected emotionally with her parents at some time in the distant past. She tries pretending that she is Jule, that she is her own mother - both women about to lose a child - while the logical part of her mind insists on telling her that this is what happens, this is normal. Children have to move on after three; they belong to the State, not to the parents, and it is the State that can give them the best foundation for a happy and successful life. This is what she has been told, but the question mark from earlier in the evening is beginning to loom even larger. As she tries to ignore the question mark, she cannot help imagining what it would be like if children remained with their parents - some would doubtlessly be less successful, but most would be— . Her mind throws up the word *happy* before she has fully finished thinking through the thought about children remaining with parents.

Is she happy? She is not completely sure. Thinking of her bag on the desk behind her, she would probably have to say no, but losing a bag, and temporarily at that, can hardly be an indicator of where one is on the happiness scale. She tries to forget about the bag, and she asks herself a second time if she is happy. The fact that she cannot come up with a definite answer worries her a little. Perhaps she is not happy; perhaps the State has failed her.

She is irritated, bored, and frustrated, and she is almost relieved when her thoughts return to the medical centre beyond the waiting room door. She picks up her train of thought from where she left it - she was looking at the circular counter in the middle of the open space - and in her mind she approaches the two women behind the counter. She is wondering whether they are receptionists or nurses when one of the women sees Thea still standing at the door and calls out brightly: 'Can I help you?

Thea takes a hasty look behind her and, seeing that there is no one else in the space, walks up to what would have to be called a reception booth or station or perhaps even an information centre - she is not at all sure how she should describe it. She is still trying to make it fit together with her memories of the place, but it is a while since she was last there, and memories tend to change and fade.

She gives the woman her number and the time of the appointment. The secretary - 'Of course, that is what she is, a secretary', thinks Thea - smiles at Thea and Thea feels like leaning across the counter and hugging her. There have not been many smiles since she entered Building C well over an hour ago.

In the capacity of a third person, viewing the inter-change, Thea feels that such an impulsive display of emotion would probably not be appreciated, and she is relieved when she sees herself asking instead, 'Busy evening?'

The secretary looks surprised. 'Not particularly,' she says, clicking through a number of screens on the computer.

Thea is aware that she is probably frowning, while, in

her mind, she is telling the secretary about her overly long wait and how she thought that there may have been an emergency.

The secretary looks up from the computer and shakes her head. She tells Thea that there have been no emergencies; in fact, she is the first client she has seen for well over an hour, possibly two.

Something is knocking furiously against Thea's brain, telling her that things are not quite right. In fact, they seem very wrong.

The secretary prints out a paper and tells Thea to take it to room six, on the right. 'The doctor will see you now,' she says and smiles a second time.

Thea takes the paper but something keeps her standing at the counter in the reception area. The secretary has already turned away and is busy with a list of figures on the computer screen.

'One more thing,' ventures Thea hesitantly.

The secretary moves her eyes away from the screen and beams encouragingly at Thea.

'It's the receptionist. The one who is in the waiting room.'

The secretary, still looking friendly and helpful, is obviously waiting for something more.

'She's not what one could call pleasant. Or helpful,' says Thea. 'And the bit in the letter about no personal effects; that just does not make any sense. And there needs to be a water— '

Thea, sitting on her uncomfortable chair in the waiting room, is wondering if she has listed all she wanted to say about the receptionist and the waiting room when the secretary interrupts her.

She raises both hands in the air. 'Wait. Wait,' and she rummages in a drawer next to her computer and hands Thea a paper. 'Form E6689. This is the form to be used for all complaints. You can complete it and leave it in the box next to door twelve, or you can post it to us - there is a box on the ground floor. Or, if you like, you can find the form online and fill it in on your PS later, when you get home.'

Wondering whether this is the case in reality, Thea watches while she takes the paper, folds it, and pushes it into one of the large pockets in her coat. Obviously she has not got her bag back, but this could be because Thea's mind is only capable of interpreting any situation from its basis in reality - and she does not have her bag. She would have been happier if she could have seen the bag hanging from her shoulder.

The secretary, however, does not seem at all upset by her comments about the receptionist; she is still smiling. Thea mumbles her thanks. The woman reminds her that the doctor is waiting.

The tablet has worked and the pain is now only a faint shadow of itself. It is getting late, and Thea seriously considers cancelling the appointment and making a new one. Perhaps she may not even have to make a new appointment; perhaps the shoulder will right itself without medication or surgery. The thought that she may not have to see a doctor at all energizes Thea. She thinks: it has to be a work-related injury, and having a break from the wheel is probably all the treatment she needs. She turns around and looks at the clock on the wall, trying to make a decision as to what she should do. Were it not for the unpleasant receptionist, it would be an easy decision to make, but the woman is an ogre, and Thea cannot imagine that she would pleasantly accept a cancellation. And if she were to go up to the desk and cancel, there is a strong chance that the woman would decide not to return her bag.

On the other hand, she feels that she has to do something: she is fed up just sitting and waiting.

While she is trying to make up her mind whether she should dare approach the woman behind her and ask to cancel her appointment, her thoughts return to Aaron.

She remembers how they both began to look forward to the irregular and infrequent meetings in the courtyard. They were never able to talk very long, but then Aaron, who got on the bus first in the morning, would sometimes mind a seat for Thea, or they would hang back in the queue of an evening, making sure that they both got on to the bus together. Thea had always loved her work, but now it took on a completely different dimension. She would wake in the morning, and as the realization of who she was and where she was replaced a diffuse world of dreams, she would remember that she was about to go to work where there was a possibility that she would see Aaron.

He fascinated her at the same time as he sometimes frightened her; she had never met anyone quite like him. Although he never openly criticized the Party, there was something in the way he said things that made Thea wonder if there was something about Unitas that she had missed. She had been brought up to believe in Unitas and what it could do for her; she had no reason to doubt what she had been told. Although the Party had never set itself up as an institution promoting either itself or some other supreme being that should be venerated, many people - Thea included - directed their need to believe in something at Unitas. Religion had been swept away decades ago; it was barely hanging on when Unitas came to power, having been rendered both insignificant and powerless by commercialism, capitalism, and technology. It was not difficult for Unitas to relegate all religions and religious practices to the area of mythology and fables. In fact, when children reached senior school they were taught a subject called Mythology and Religion where the emphasis was on the implausibility of all myths and belief patterns. Children were taught that such stories had evolved over time as a way of combating widespread feelings of insecurity. With Unitas, there was no insecurity, so it logically followed that such practices and beliefs were no longer necessary.

But people need to believe in something. Commercialism, and even narcissism to a point, had been obliterated along with religion; as a result, people automatically looked around for something else in which they could believe. Thea's belief in the Party is strong - without Unitas she is quite sure that she would not be where she is now. She would not have received such an in-depth education; she would not have the security of assured employment and accommodation. She would probably have had to fend for herself: she had read books about life before Unitas, when society seemed to have been made up of a few winners and many losers. She was always thankful that she had had the good fortune to be born when she had been born. But, when she listened to Aaron speaking, she sometimes wondered if she had misunderstood things. Such thoughts were ever only on the periphery of her mind, and she did not give them a lot of credence; however, they were there, and they refused to go away. She told herself that it was not that Aaron was in any way critical of the Party, but that he was simply looking at it, and everything associated with it, from another perspective - a perspective that she had never considered.

Until she met Aaron, she had not spoken with anyone who did not wholeheartedly agree with everything the Party was doing: Unitas is there for each and every one of them, and they are there for the Party. Of course Jule is upset about her daughter, but, underneath all the ranting and the tears, Thea is almost certain that Jule agrees with her - that Unitas knows best. They have absolutely no reason to doubt what the Party does or how it does it: Unitas is for everyone; it is a uniting factor that makes the whole flourish and prosper. Political systems that concentrate on the individual parts usually flounder and eventually become corrupted and die. Thea has nothing with which she could compare Unitas, but she trusts the Party and she believes everything that she is told.

Part of her mind, however, refuses to let go of Jule and her child. If she is honest with herself, she is no longer completely sure that Jule believes that Unitas knows best.

Aaron, on the other hand, had his own way of looking at things, and Thea was alarmed and even strangely excited that it was possible to have an independent way of looking at the world, the political situation, and, most of all, Unitas. As he talked, and as she listened, she wondered if there were other people who thought the same way as he did and said the same things as he did. She had never questioned Unitas - it was, after all, what life was all about - but now she was beginning to wonder. When Aaron talked about the individual and the importance of individual thought, her mind had tried to disassociate what he was saying from the mantra that had been the backbone of her entire existence - that the whole was more important than its parts; that society must always come before the individual.

Then one evening, on impulse, Thea did not get off at her stop but remained on the bus and got off with Aaron at his stop, not far from the centre of the sector.

There are only six people left in the waiting room, and as the clock on the wall behind the receptionist ticks slowly towards eight, the room takes on a weary, end-of-the-day look. The empty chairs seem even more empty as it becomes obvious that no one else will be using them that evening; the few people left look tired and dejected - like objects left on stalls at the end of market day. A bald man with glasses, sitting in the back row, stands up with a sense of relief as his number is called and hurries to the door at the front of the room. The remaining people sigh and move slightly on the uncomfortable aqua chairs, each of them possibly thinking about things beyond the room or things in the room that they cannot change.

The lack of windows, the bright light, and the absence of any external sound make it difficult for the people in the waiting room to correctly estimate the time of day - all they know is that they have been there a long time, and when they turn around and look at the clock, they can see that it is almost eight o'clock.

When Thea turns around - as she does from time to time - she is very aware of her bag still sitting on the receptionist's desk. She is thinking of the PS that could have made the evening go just that little bit more quickly; she is also wondering why personal effects are not allowed. It really makes no sense. Having nothing else to do, her thoughts tend to run rampant, rushing off in one direction and then, for no reason at all, joining up with other thoughts and moving in a completely different direction. Her head is beginning to ache, and she knows that it would help if she could breathe in some fresh air; it would also help if there was something else to look at, not just four uninteresting, pale yellow walls. While she thinks of fresh air, and things to look at, she is also thinking of what she will do when she finally leaves Building C.

Thinking about leaving Building C pushes her thoughts back to her fantasy about the medical centre and the appointment for which she has been waiting so long. She watches as the figure that is herself walks away from the counter in the middle of the space and makes its way to room six. She sees herself knocking hesitantly on the door and is somehow aware of a far-away voice telling her to enter.

The doctor - at first irritatingly undefined - eventually comes into focus as a small, rotund man with balding hair and a white doctor's coat. He is sitting behind a large mahogany desk that manages to both establish his importance and dwarf him physically. Thea is thinking about the conflict inherent in these two ideas when he motions the person who is Thea to a chair in front of the desk, places his fingertips together and asks, 'Well, young lady, how can I help you?'

Thea is not sure if that is what a doctor would say - perhaps the term *young lady* could be easily misconstrued as too familiar, or too childish. After all, she is twenty-two and the doctor is meeting her in a professional capacity. She rolls back the film in her head and hears the doctor asking, '3325-678? How can I help you?'

Wondering if the question is now just a little too formal, she is on the verge of adding 'this evening?' but thinks better of it and focuses instead on the image of the doctor. She is captivated by his stature, the way he is holding his fingers, and the high polish on his desk. She tries to bring her thoughts back to why she is in the room, and she watches while her virtual double tells him about the pain, throwing out questions as to its likely cause - a pulled muscle, bursitis, tendinitis, or even cancer?

While Thea can feel herself putting words into her own mouth, she is aware of herself talking about throwing and wedging, and trying to explain how heavy and resilient clay is before it has been coaxed into something that resembles the mug on his desk. She goes on to explain about all the repetitive movements. She asks him again if it could be cancer. Thea, sitting in the waiting room with her eyes closed, urges herself on.

From what Thea can see, the doctor does not interrupt, but sits patiently, his fingertips still forming a roof top (or is it a church steeple?), his eyes fixed on her face. When she asks him a second time if he thinks it could be cancer, he shakes his head, stands up, and comes around to the front of his desk.

She watches while she removes her coat and jumper, and the doctor carefully slides a small flat disc back and forth over her shoulder, asking her where the pain is, whether it hurts more in one place than in another, then returns to his desk and connects the disc to his screen. He motions Thea to pass her PB in front of the screen, and the display quickly fills with all her details, including a recent photo. There is a few seconds of inactivity, and then a new window appears, covering all her personal information with lines and lines of text, no doubt relating to her shoulder, complete with several diagrams and illustrations.

In her mind, she watches while the doctor studies the results. 'Bursitis. I thought as much,' he says, as he quickly scrolls through some of the text. 'Rest and special exercises - it's all there.' He pushes aside his swivel chair and begins to prepare an injection. 'If it doesn't get better, come back and see me,' he says. 'You may need another injection, perhaps several.'

Thea thinks that this is what she has suspected all along, and then she wonders if she is possibly putting words into the doctor's mouth, creating the scenario that she wants, not the one that is real.

While she is trying to decide how much is simply wishful thinking, the doctor wipes the injection site with an antiseptic and then slowly injects the cortisone into Thea's shoulder, telling her that it could take anything up to a couple of days before it starts to work.

Even though she cannot physically feel anything, she imagines that the injection must result in a piercing, burning pain. Thinking about the sharp piece of steel cutting into her flesh, she almost has to fight against the impulse to cry out. But there is no real pain, only perceived pain. While she is grappling with what is real and what is not, she is experiencing a feeling of elation that her colleague's fears of 'something really serious' are completely unfounded. Well, possibly. That is the scenario that she is hoping for and it makes sense that it is part of what she is imagining.

The doctor is finished, and Thea believes that he is probably talking - a rounding-off of the appointment. No doubt there is information about a follow-up appointment, and a reminder about exercises and the importance of rest.

She watches herself pulling on her jumper with some effort and continues watching while she wriggles back into her coat. Her exhilaration at receiving such a benign and simple diagnosis threatens to inflate her like some kind of helium balloon - she can already see herself rising up from the floor and floating around the room. She makes sure that the figure who is herself thanks the doctor several times, and then, wondering whether she is the last patient for the evening, she leaves room six.

She breathes out, hoping that her fantasy will match reality. She has had a feeling all along that the shoulder pain is really nothing serious and she is clinging to the doctor's diagnosis of bursitis, even if his diagnosis is simply a reflection of what she desperately wants to hear.

She is fully aware that the doctor and his room and even the secretary were not real, but she also knows that attitudes and expectations are so tied up with reality that, at times, it is difficult to know where the one begins and the other ends. Although she has never made a study of it, she believes that precognition is possible: it is all a matter of being open to things. If she believes, really believes, that her pain is caused by cancer, then there is a good chance that it will be, and if she believes that it is something simple, then that is just as likely. The doctor she will eventually see may not look the same as the doctor in room six, but it is quite possible that he or she will come to the same conclusion and that the same treatment will be recommended. For Thea, everything begins in the mind; it is like a crossroads with many options. The direction, she has always argued, is completely up to each and every individual.

Another man is called to the door, and Thea sighs audibly as she realizes that she has been overlooked, yet again. But then, she argues diplomatically, if they are running late, they are running late with everyone, so perhaps it is not a case of being overlooked. For whatever reason, the appointment schedule is not working: they need to allow more time for each appointment and calculate with having fewer patients each day. If she had her bag, and could access her PS, she would be writing up a list of things to complain about once she leaves the waiting room.

Her thoughts stop at the word *writing*; the word itself is a leftover from another time. She has heard that many, many decades ago it was something that was done on paper, or some other surface, usually using pens or pencils, but then computers and electronic devices appeared, and people began to tap out their messages on keyboards or screens. From what Thea had heard, pens and paper were still being used during this transition into electronic communication, but they were already on the wane. By the time Unitas took over, very few people used pens or paper; in fact, there were not many people who knew how to write. Eventually, writing became a curiosity - an elitist hobby.

But the word itself remained, and the action of storing information on a PS, or even transferring information from one PS to another, is still occasionally referred to as writing. Thea does own a pen, and she knows how to use it, but she is happy that she is able to interact with her PS through a mixture of speech and gesture. She thinks how easy it is to be able to slide her finger over a screen, and how difficult it must have been when non-spoken communication was limited to a pen and paper. Her thought hesitates over the word *non-spoken,* as she speculates that there is no such thing any longer.

When she entered the waiting room, she had noted the receptionist's pen on her desk, and wondered if it was simply a keepsake or some kind of link with the past, but had then seen that the receptionist used it to write patients' numbers on the small pieces of paper. She finds the idea of the receptionist writing anything on small pieces of paper quite absurd, but decides that it could simply be her way of coping with being the receptionist.

Thea thinks of her own pen somewhere in her bag on the receptionist's desk, and she thinks of the odd words and phrases she writes in a notebook she once found in an antique shop. Getting her fingers to hold the pen properly and shape the letters was difficult at first, but, in many ways, writing is not so unlike using a brush to decorate pieces of pottery, and she likes the idea of being able to do something that not everyone else can do.

Her thoughts move from pen, paper, and letters to the fact that she is becoming more and more frustrated with the long wait. She is not very patient at the best of times, and sitting in an enclosed waiting room for more than two hours is most assuredly not something she would normally sign up for. While she is thinking about all of this, and feeling extremely frustrated, any connection between the waiting room and the doctors beyond suddenly evaporates, and all she is left with is an impervious wall. She thinks of fairy stories where valiant princes must fight their way through similar walls made of tangled, thorny bushes, all in an attempt to save some beautiful princess being held prisoner in the solitary and dismal castle beyond the wall.

Her thoughts move away from the image of richly clad princes cutting their way through impenetrable brambles, and she watches the man approaching the door and then disappearing from view. She wonders if she is right about the layout beyond the door and whether there are twelve separate rooms or whether there are only a couple. She sighs and her thoughts return to Aaron.

It was tenderly warm and still quite light when they stepped off the bus. Shadows from the tall administrative buildings had begun to cut their way between buildings and across streets towards Aaron's house, where they were already merging into slabs of multi-toned grey. The house itself was small and unimposing, and, looking at it from the street, Thea correctly guessed that it probably had two bedrooms and a small living room. As they walked up the short path to the front door, she wondered if there was a closed-in verandah at the back. She had seen such verandahs on other pre-Change houses, and she had fallen in love with them straight away. The idea of being inside and outside at the same time appealed to her, especially if the outside included a garden with trees and flowers.

Aaron's garden was simple with many leafy bushes and a few colourful flowers forming an edge to the two rectangles of green grass on each side of the path, but for Thea, who lived in one of the tower blocks, it was wonderful. Even the irregular stone path leading to the front door grabbed her attention, and she would have liked to have asked about the brick-red and yellow-orange stones - where they had come from and if they had always had just that shape - but she felt that they were possibly questions that should wait until a later visit.

The front door opened into a short, dark, timber hall with four doors, two on each side. On either side of the front door were elongated stained-glass windows, distorting and colouring the late afternoon light as it drew lines across the timber flooring. Thea thought of glazes bringing her pottery to life, and she also thought of the light from the setting sun turning the river into a canvas of reds and oranges and yellows.

The first two doors led to bedrooms, while the next door on the left was to a bathroom, and the door on the right led into a cosy living room. At the end of the hall was the kitchen and next to the kitchen a small laundry and the back door. To Thea's delight, the back door led out on to a closed-in back verandah.

By the time Unitas finally came to power, human genome editing was widespread; in fact, it was so widespread that it was considered the norm. Beginning decades before as a way of eliminating certain diseases, the process was first hailed as a major scientific milestone. Children who most probably would have developed illnesses such as cancer, immunity disorders, cystic fibrosis, and diabetes remained disease-free because of the intervention of science at the embryonic stage. Although there were many who agreed that such intervention was to be applauded, there were others who felt that playing God was playing with fire. No one knew what the effects of this manipulation would be further down the track, in the next generation or in generations that were so far into the future they could not even be properly imagined. The people who opposed this science were concerned by the fact that humans were actually altering DNA, the very cornerstone of life. Although they could accept that children and adults should be able to lead healthy lives, they were hesitant about the measures taken to secure such a goal. Apart from no one knowing how such manipulated genes might behave in the future, there was also the question of ethics.

Despite all the opposition, genetic engineering to eliminate disease became so mainstream that after a number of years most people did not even question it. Medical journals, and even mainstream social media, lauded the brains behind such an innovative solution to society's health problems. The man and the woman who had together shown that it was possible were awarded the Nobel Prize in Medicine.

But after that first enormous step had been taken into the realm of the gods, it did not take long before people were pushing the possibilities even further. No longer satisfied with simply eradicating certain diseases, the scientists began to look at other areas of DNA. If it was possible to control disease, then it should also be possible to control things like appearance and intellect. Some parents might want a strong, well-built footballer with dark hair; others might prefer a petite blue-eyed ballerina. Thinking of future career possibilities for their children, many parents saw the advantages of being able to create a child who would be a genius at maths or music, or who would show unusual artistic talent or a natural aptitude for business. The scientists began to realize that this was all possible; everything could be arranged - it was simply a matter of re-sorting the genetic mix.

Once again the opposition, remembering the criticism that had been directed at genetic engineering all those decades ago, raised its head and reminded everyone that it was an ethical question, but by now very few people were listening. In an age where people were completely focused on themselves, the option of being able to choose the 'perfect' child to go with the perfect lifestyle was far too tempting to ignore. Several genetic modification companies had wedged themselves into the market at the very beginning of the trend, and within only a few years had expanded exponentially. Religion was already on its way out, and no one was particularly interested in ethics, especially not the people ordering the designer children and the companies raking in the money.

When Unitas stepped into government, many things about human genetic engineering changed - or, at least, began to move in a completely different direction. An organization like Unitas that was focused on the whole before the individual was not interested in designer children, but it could see ways of using the science for its own purposes.

While Unitas was still establishing itself as the ultimate ruler and stringent regulations were being laid down, every person in the country between the ages of sixteen and sixty was called to an interview and an assessment. This was a mammoth task and it took almost two years to complete, but once the framework was in place assessments were done only when a person reached the age of sixteen. These people, neither children nor adults, were called to an interview at the Department of

Cohabitation and Population in their sector - an exercise which usually necessitated a whole day. The exceedingly meticulous evaluation included an interview by a board of three Cohabitation and Population officers, as well as genetic screening, and thorough medical and psychological examinations. There was also a ten-page questionnaire that sought to establish not only intelligence levels but also weaknesses and aptitudes. Any weaknesses or strengths - genetic, intellectual, and social - were highlighted, and, at the end of the process, the individual was informed as to whether or not he or she would be permitted to reproduce. This was an assessment where there was no room for discussion; the decision of the Department was final. Those deemed unfit for procreation would be given a date and time for sterilization - same building, different floor - after which their PB would be updated with the letter X for 'infertile'. Those who passed the assessment would have their PB marked O for 'fertile'. Why the selection of the letters X and O had been made was a mystery to all except those who had chosen the letters. Within a short period of the government being in power, people became very aware that they belonged to either the X group or the O group. Although Unitas was aiming for total equality, there was a feeling of elitism in the O group, a feeling that was never verbalized but which was there anyway.

The Party hoped that by culling the mentally weak, the

carriers of possible diseases, and those with criminal tendencies or unacceptable ideas, it would, eventually, be able to create the perfect society. It was not interested in producing rugged athletes or piano-playing beauties; it was totally focused on the whole picture. The cosmetic genetic modification businesses disappeared the moment Unitas came to power, as did many other businesses. The era of the individual as a consumer had come to a sudden and definite end.

As far as Unitas was concerned, its aim was not necessarily to control relationships but, instead, to control the result of these relationships. Once people had been divided into X and O camps, the only group that really held any interest for Unitas was the O group.

All relationships within the O group were carefully monitored for physical, intellectual, and emotional compatibility. If a relationship was approved, the man and the woman would be called to the Department of Cohabitation and Population, twenty-fifth floor, where eggs and sperm would be collected and the embryos so created would then be gene-edited. The Party had no intention of taking any risks - by abolishing the sexual act's role in reproduction, it put itself completely and unreservedly in control.

Neither Thea nor Aaron were giving any thought to the Department of Cohabitation and Population or to the division of the population into X and O. Had anyone ventured to ask them to which of these two camps they belonged, they would most probably have looked a little puzzled, confused even, and they would both have answered that they had O on their PB. Then it is most likely that they may have frowned or turned away, indicating that a line had been drawn against any further questions.

They said very little as they walked though the house, their footsteps softly echoing on the timber floors; their smiles and nods, as Aaron opened doors to show Thea the rooms behind them, were unassuming and somewhat self-conscious. Thea was already beginning to wonder if she had done the right thing in following Aaron home: they were, after all, only colleagues; they scarcely knew each other. She wondered how he interpreted her action, and she blushed as she understood that he may have read more into it than she had intended.

She said: 'I just wanted to see where you live. Stupid really, I suppose; I can't stay very long.' and almost as soon as the words had hit the air around her, she regretted that she had let them escape.

Aaron smiled and then waved his hand in the air as though he understood her anxiety and her regret and was helping to dissipate the offending words as quickly as possible. 'Of course,' he said, 'I understand.'

Aaron's house, although within easy walking distance of the centre, was fortunately without a view of the administrative buildings, and, once inside, it was almost possible to pretend that the administrative buildings, and indeed the Party itself, did not exist. Aaron closed the curtains in the living room, switched on the overhead light, and, sliding a heavy-looking cabinet a metre or so towards the centre of the room, indicated to Thea a hidden bookcase. The bookcase had been recessed into the wall, where books, many of them possibly unavailable for decades, stood silently in the darkness, no doubt waiting for someone to read them.

The books were in a variety of sizes. A few were hard-backs with colourful dust jackets but most were paperbacks, and although a number seemed very old and even fragile, the majority appeared to be in perfect condition. Thea gasped, realizing that she was looking at a treasure trove of literature. Glancing at the titles, she was aware that although some of the books were books that she had seen before, many were completely unknown to her. She guessed that there were possibly even a number of banned books - impossible to get hold of and extremely dangerous to own.

They had stopped printing books long before the Change, but for a while at least there had still been a variety of printed books to be found in second-hand shops and private collections. Once Unitas came to power, books that could possibly incite oppositional thought or rebellion or even ordinary intellectual curiosity were withdrawn from digital publication, and all printed copies were removed from the few libraries - usually connected to universities or museums - that still remained, and, wherever possible, private book collections. Occasionally Unitas made surprise raids on units and homes, and sometimes the raids were successful. Lists of the forbidden books were drawn up and sent to everyone's PS on a regular basis; it was stressed that people who were in possession of any such books were to hand them in to any of the Administration buildings. People were also encouraged to report anyone whom they suspected might be hiding banned books.

Although the people in power did their best to destroy as many books as possible, they were well aware of the difficulties surrounding such an eradication - there would always be some copies that would evade discovery - but they were not unduly concerned: nowadays most people did all their reading on their PS, where all reading matter was very carefully monitored by the Party. If a few people managed to read *Animal Farm* or *The Children of Men*, it was probably not going to mean the end of the Party, and, in all likelihood, the people themselves would eventually be found out.

Though Thea was delighted to see many titles that she recognized from her own reading, both on her PS and in book form, she was excited to see so many titles she did not recognize. She ran her fingers along the spines of the books, delighting in the feel of them, and at one point she leant closer to the shelves and breathed in the special book smell, something she could never have with her PS. She picked out a few books at random - *The Road*, *Spycatcher*, *We*, *Fahrenheit 451*, *The Outline of History*, *Never Let Me Go*, *The Giver* - looking at each in turn, flicking through the pages, reading the blurb on the back and then returning each book carefully to its place on the shelf. Most of these titles were unknown to her, although she had a feeling that she had seen some of them on the lists of banned books. Whether she knew what she was looking at or not, she was ecstatic, and she kept throwing Aaron looks of disbelief and delight. She had never seen so many books collected together in one space. She had a few physical books of her own, but they were all titles that were approved of by the State. Like everyone else, she did the majority of her reading on her PS.

Eventually it struck her that she could not stay standing where she was indefinitely; taking one last look at all the books, as if in an effort to imprint the sight and smell of them for ever on her mind, she turned around and stepped back out into the room.

While Aaron returned the cabinet to its original

position and straightened the hand-woven mat in front of it, Thea, still thinking about what she had seen, walked slowly across the room and dropped her bag on to the nearest sofa. Then she turned just as Aaron finished straightening the mat. Her ineffectual, self-conscious words had dissolved and disappeared somewhere within the confines of the house; she was no longer aware of them, but the house, the books - even the closed-in verandah - had sent Thea's thoughts racing in new directions.

Thea had always argued that Life, with all its ups and downs and twists and turns, was never simply something that just happened; it was always skilfully orchestrated by Unitas, which, like some supreme god-like being, directed the mechanics of the society in which she lived. She accepted this manipulation, because she trusted the Party and she was certain that it knew best. Someone had to be steering society along the right path, and the fact that this was so made her feel assured and safe. But Aaron had told her that her ideas about life and direction and even security were illogical and badly thought through. Beneath the ironclad umbrella of Unitas there may have been a degree of regulated certainty, but there was no room for each individual to freely seek his or her own path. As he put it on more than one occasion, there was no freedom, neither for the individual nor for life itself. Everything was regimented to the will of the Party.

Thea had retorted saying that it was really of no importance, because it was obvious that the Party had to know best. Aaron had not deemed her response worthy of a reply - he had looked at her for a moment and had then shaken his head and changed the subject.

Standing in Aaron's house, she remembered clearly what she had said and how he had then looked at her, and she wondered if there was a slight possibility that she could be wrong and that he was right. Perhaps Unitas was not really offering freedom - not the kind that Aaron was talking about - and perhaps the Party *was* all about regulation and control. If she were to even begin considering this possibility, it would mean turning everything on its head, and she was not sure if she could cope with the enormity of such an about-turn.

Thea is thinking back to the time spent in Aaron's house; she is also thinking how, as the final rays of the sun were disappearing behind buildings, and street lights were flickering into life, she had said goodbye to Aaron and, picking up her bag, had quietly let herself out by the front door. Even as she left the house, she had still been thinking about different perspectives and what might or might not be true. She had desperately wanted to hang on to what she had always believed about Unitas, but, even as she clung to her beliefs, she could see and feel them slowly disintegrating beneath her fingers. Thinking back, she wondered if anything was any longer the way she had always believed it to be.

Or was there a possibility that it was Aaron who was wrong and that it was she who was right?

She was confused. Right from the beginning she had found Aaron attractive, but it was his mind that had fascinated her most of all. Other men she knew had the same ideas and beliefs as she had: they all looked up to the Party and were able to spout the right words and phrases at any given time; they did not seem to give any thought to freedom and how it might be interpreted. It was as though they had never really thought about the ideas behind Unitas, the concepts that motivated the reasons for its existence. She had never thought like this before; she, like everyone else she knew, simply accepted everything she had been told. But what if part of what she had been told was wrong? What if there was another way of living - a way that concentrated more on the individual than the whole?

She pulled herself up with a start; she had finally thought the unthinkable - that the individual might be more important than the whole - and now that the thought had been released, she knew that there was no way that she would be able to move it back into its Pandora's box.

After leaving Aaron's house, she had suddenly become concerned that someone might have seen her, but the street had seemed totally deserted, and she was quite certain that she saw no one. Even though their relationship had barely tilted over into a state that could be termed in any way serious, she knew that all O people had to advise the Department of Cohabitation and Population of any liaison with another O person, however platonic. The Department would then decide, on the basis of the individual assessments, if the two people involved could be given permission to continue seeing each other. Most of the time there was no problem - the two individuals having already passed all the controls and been considered suitable for reproduction - but Unitas liked to be holding all the strings; not for a moment were people permitted to believe that the choice was all theirs.

Up until very recently, Thea had accepted that Unitas, in the guise of the Department of Cohabitation and Population, should be so very involved in what she did and who she met. This involvement was, after all, for the betterment of the society in which she lived, but now she was not so sure. While her thoughts rotated in a number of unruly circles, some of them intersecting, she just hoped that her visit to Aaron had remained completely off the radar. Once his street was well and truly behind her, and she was in sight of her own long line of tower blocks, she began to relax and even feel amazed that everything had all gone so smoothly.

Though now she is no longer certain that it *had* gone quite that smoothly.

The following day Aaron was on the bus, but the seat next to him was already taken, and she did not get to speak with him. During her break, she stood in the courtyard, hoping that he would turn up as he often did, but he did not. She consoled herself, remembering that he did not always have the time, or an excuse, to come down to the factory, or perhaps, she decided, he was simply taking precautions. She tried to take heart with the thought that she would see him on the bus in the evening, but he was not in the queue when everyone lined up at the bus stop after work. Even now, sitting in the waiting room, she can remember the overwhelming feeling of fear that began to seep through her, almost paralysing her, when she arrived at the bus stop and was unable to find him. It was at that point that she would have liked to have been able to turn the clock back, but she knew it was impossible.

She must have dozed off; in fact, she is still not sure whether she is asleep or awake. All she knows is that she is back in room six at the Medical Centre. The small round doctor is seated once again behind his impressive desk, and he is talking to her. She can see the diagrams and some of the text on his screen, but it is at an angle so she cannot read it properly. He is talking to her, while his eyes are fixed on the screen.

'It's quite clear,' he is saying, his hands moving in a circle between the screen and the table. 'What you have is definitely a dislocation.' He turns the screen towards Thea and points to a scan of her shoulder. 'You can see here that the joint is not sitting as it should, and there is quite a lot of inflammation in the area.'

Thea leans forward, not sure of what she should be looking at. She nods politely, wondering if a dislocation with inflammation is anything to worry about.

He turns the screen back towards himself and peers at it for a few seconds. He is saying something about nerves and blood supply when the image flickers and turns black. When Thea is next aware of the doctor he is talking about lungs and cancer and how shoulder pain can be a symptom.

'Not my area of expertise, I'm afraid,' he says before speaking a few sentences into his screen. You'll have to see someone in the cancer section.'

Thea shakes her head vigorously and opens her eyes.

She feels that she can accept a dislocation, but certainly not cancer. She wants to force her thoughts back to the original diagnosis, but everything has broken up, and, try as she may, she cannot retrieve that image of room six and the plump little doctor. She turns her head and looks at the clock, telling herself that it is her imagination that is running wild and that everything is going to be okay.

Thea's thoughts slip back to Aaron. She has been telling herself for days that there is a logical explanation and that he will eventually turn up. While she is worrying about where he is, she imagines seeing him on the bus, or being surprised by his turning up suddenly in the courtyard. In these make-believe scenarios she asks him where he has been, but he merely smiles and puts his finger to his lips and quickly changes the subject. In other images, he talks about an unscheduled trip to another sector, or a bout of 'flu. His absence is most probably fully explainable and normal, and she wonders why she is so worried.

Her thoughts return to the consultation rooms beyond the waiting room. She remembers how she had imagined seeing a doctor and how, when she first saw him, he had given her the diagnosis she had been expecting - nothing serious. She has decided to ignore the two later diagnoses, and she picks up her daydream at the point where she leaves the doctor's surgery and is once again back in the open space. She would have expected to have seen other patients or clients emerging from consulting rooms or even from the waiting room, but, as before, there is no one anywhere. Further away, in the centre of the area, she can see the two secretaries, but otherwise the place is completely devoid of people - patients or otherwise. The thought goes through her head that she could easily add a few people - it is, after all, her story. She needs some answers, but there is no one around who can give them to her, unless, of course, she makes them up. She walks up to what she has mentally designated as the command centre and catches the attention of the pleasant secretary.

The woman, who is now sorting papers, has not suddenly become less pleasant while Thea was seeing the doctor, and she looks up and asks Thea if everything is okay. Can she help her with something?

Thea is aware that she nods; in her mind, words, forming a question, move around and then come together: 'A tall man. Dark hair, glasses. Is it possible that you may have seen him? Probably around seven-thirty.'

For a moment the secretary appears to be thinking, but she then shakes her head.'Not that I can remember,' she says. 'You don't happen to have his number?'

It was an obvious question, but Thea was not expecting it. She tries to put herself back more than an hour to when the receptionist called out the man's number. At the time she had no reason to memorize the number, but the digits *44 something* keep coming into her mind. She wonders if the last three digits could be 446 or 449 or... She wishes that she had been more attentive.

In Thea's mind the secretary has clicked on a new screen, and then she asks if the man is a close friend. She tells Thea that they normally do not hand out information about other clients.

Thea thinks: No, he's not a friend - but he could be. She continues, 'I mean, I had never seen him before; he was just kind to me. In the waiting room.'

The secretary does not seem to be daunted by the fact that Thea does not know the man; instead she flicks through several screens and shakes her head. 'I'm awfully sorry, but no one with any of those number combinations has passed through here today.'

Thea is pretty sure about the 44 even if she cannot remember the rest of the number. She thinks that it makes no sense that no one with that number - or that part of a number - has passed through the centre. She remembers hearing the receptionist and then watching the man walk through the door.

As if the secretary has heard her thoughts, she shrugs and returns her computer screen to the main menu.

Thea is not about to give up. She asks, 'Perhaps you remember a man, a bald man with glasses?'

Once again the secretary smiles patiently. 'As I said before, you were the first client for more than an hour; it has been a very slow day here today, and, to tell you the truth, I'm looking forward to finishing at nine.'

Thea can hear the woman, but the voice seems to be getting further and further away, a bit like a scream disappearing down a tunnel, or perhaps like a flock of birds flying across a field towards a forest of dark trees. She is feeling light-headed and cold; like the birds, she is moving towards something that is both dark and enveloping. She knows that she should sit down. Something is telling her that she is going to faint. She takes a quick look, but there are no chairs, not anywhere. She begins to say something to the woman behind the charcoal-glass counter, but there is no counter, just an expanse of black water, and the woman is floating, or is she being held up by birds? Before she can arrange the words in any kind of sensible order, she loses consciousness and collapses in a green heap on the floor.

Watching herself collapse in a heap, even if it is in her mind, has shaken Thea a little, and she wonders whether it is such a good idea to be fantasizing about what might, or might not, happen on the other side of the door. There are a multitude of possibilities, and there is no way that she can follow every possibility to its likely or unlikely conclusion. She wonders to what extent her fears and anxieties are creating the many scenarios, both beyond the door and in the waiting room itself.

The evening is grinding on. Thea's gaze, which has been restlessly moving around the room and across the few people still patiently waiting, comes to rest on a woman sitting in front of her, a few chairs to her right. The woman appears to be around forty, and she is dressed entirely in black: black skin-tight trousers, black jumper, and, as far as Thea can see without falling off her chair, black shoes. As well, the woman has shoulder-length black hair without a touch of grey. She is probably medium height, on the thin side of slim, and Thea can easily imagine her jumping to her feet and beginning a gymnastics or, perhaps, yoga session. The more Thea thinks of this rather insane possibility, the more she feels it would be a good idea. She really needs to be moving her body and stretching; if she dared, she would get up from her chair and take a few turns around the room. Her thoughts swing through several different levels of awareness to long-distance plane trips when it is of utmost importance to spend time in the on-board gym or, at the very least, to stand up occasionally and walk around the plane. Information leaflets handed out after boarding indicate what exercises should be done to loosen muscles and retain a regular blood flow. The gym attendants reiterate the same message; obviously the receptionist knows nothing about long-distance plane travel.

Thea is not much of an expert either. She has only ever been on a plane twice, and both times the trips were work-related and concerned international ceramic fairs. She remembers that the words *The Practical and the Beautiful* were used to describe one of these fairs, and the ceramics factory from Sector 24781 had had work on display. She travelled with a small, hand-picked group from the factory, and, with a slight, involuntary shudder, she remembers how the plane trip was preceded by months of interviews, questionnaires, applications, and, finally, after she had been approved, the stern talk given by one of the senior officers from Administration. They would be monitored throughout the entire trip, and one step out of line would result in severe penalties. They were not told what form these penalties would take; it was simply left to their own imagination.

At the time she did not reflect on the severity of the application process: it was simply the way things were done. There had to be rules and regulations, otherwise society would disintegrate; she had been told this so many times - she had no reason to believe otherwise. It was a special privilege to be able to travel abroad, and she was grateful that she had been allowed to have the experience.

Thinking back to the fair, she realizes that she had spent all her time with the people from her sector and that she had had very little to do with anyone else. She remembers watching the throngs of people, wondering what they were thinking - if they were happy. Unitas had impressed upon her, and everyone else, that only people living in a society where the whole was more important than the individual could experience real happiness. She had felt a little sorry for the people milling around her at the fair, the people she did not know - the people who believed that the individual was more important than the whole of society.

She returns to the present and makes a mental note. Another thing to mention once she leaves the waiting room: a definite need for exercise or, at the very least, permission to walk around the room. She finds it amazing that a Health and Wellness department is not aware of this - it should be part of their general patient plan.

The woman in black stretches her arms above her head and then rolls her shoulders several times. Thea can feel the woman's stress reflected back into her own body, and for a moment she feels very much at one with the woman.

Thea has not often felt at one with anyone. The homes she grew up in discouraged children from forming close relationships with each other - if two children were seen to be best friends, one of them would always be moved to another home, in a completely different sector. When Thea was ten, she was moved after she and another little girl - Thea can no longer remember her number - were seen to be too close. The other little girl, freckles and red plaits, was very much the same as Thea - impulsive, forthright, and slightly original. It was only natural that the two children should have gravitated towards each other when everything and everyone around them was so unimaginative and regimented. Not that ten-year-old Thea then gave much thought to the lack of imagination - as far as she was concerned, this is how life was; she had nothing with which she could compare her situation. She very quickly learnt that having best friends went against the idea of a whole, uniform society.

One of the things Unitas fears most is close-knit friendships: two people who make a practice of discussing their ideas and thoughts with each other can very quickly become three or four or five, or even more, all of them sharing the same secrets, the same ideas, the same grudges, and the same resentment. A small group of people can be in complete agreement with the ideas central to Unitas or - and this is the Party's greatest fear - it can be a group of people in opposition to everything that Unitas stands for. The Party has done much to rid itself of opposition at government level, but it is not so naïve that it believes that everyone agrees with the changes that have been made. Admittedly, most of the changes were made quite some time ago, but there are still people who remember what it had been like before the Change, and the Party knows that among those people who remember there are some who still resent what has happened. Unitas cannot afford for this resentment to twist around others; while the Party silently quashes children's attempts to team up with like-minded souls, it stridently lauds the principle of everyone acting for the whole of society, pointing out how much progress has been made since the individual's needs were subjugated to allow *everyone* to focus on the needs of the whole.

The government is not being fearful without reason. There have already been a couple of rebellions, both of which were put down without too much inconvenience, but the fact that there are people in the society who are prepared to rebel makes Unitas even more cautious and even more restrictive. Thea remembers, when she was about twelve, how a small group of people had managed to enter the Department of Administration and Justice when there was a board meeting in session. No one knew how they managed to get past both the guards and the surveillance cameras, but they did. They even reached the boardroom on the top floor, where they detonated a home-made bomb. One of the board members was killed in the blast, which seriously injured two of his colleagues, before security guards burst into the room and killed two of the rebels. The remaining four became the subject of a series of rumours. Some people said they had been tried and then executed; others claimed that they were still alive but had been imprisoned somewhere in isolation; still others were adamant that they had been given brain-altering surgery and that they were now in a home for the mentally deranged.

No matter what happened to the rebels themselves, the media, adroitly manipulated by the Party, assured the people that they were now safe, that Unitas had protected them and would continue to protect them from such violent and illogical acts. Articles extolling the virtues and self-sacrifice of the Party were streamed to everyone's PS, and by the end of the week there were very few who did not doubt that the Party had been cruelly targeted.

Thea remembers the sense of relief she had felt when the supervisor of the home had told the children that there was no longer any cause to worry and that everyone was safe.

Her thoughts are wandering again, and she tries to pick up the strands of what she was thinking earlier about the overweight doctor and his surgery. She remembers that his first diagnosis was positive, and that she had left his room feeling relieved and energized. Then she remembers that she fainted or fell. She tries to remember what it was that happened to her after she left the surgery. Part of her brain is telling her to forget it, that it is simply her imagination playing tricks on her, while another part of her brain is suggesting that dreams and daydreams can often give us an understanding of that which lies before us.

She would like to know exactly what is lying before her.

Although she cannot clearly remember exactly what happened earlier - did she faint or did she simply fall? - she has a feeling that, on some imaginary level, she is now lying on a narrow examination table in a small room. The ceiling is white as are the walls; for a very brief moment, as the image becomes clearer and as her other self begins to regain consciousness, she wonders whether she might be floating on, or in, a cloud. Becoming more aware of her surroundings, she understands that she must be in one of the other consulting rooms, for although the room looks very similar to what she remembers about room six, there is no portly doctor and no mahogany desk. She tries to work out why she should be lying on a table in an examination room - from what she can remember, she has already seen the doctor.

Thea applies brakes to her train of thought. Perhaps these fantasies or images or daydreams are simply a sign of her confusion and her irritation with the receptionist. The idea that they might give her a glimpse of the future is ridiculous to say the least. She is angry and tired and extremely worried about her arm.

She focuses her attention on the pale yellow walls and tries to forget the plump doctor, the Medical Centre, the diagnosis, and herself lying on a narrow examination table. But the thoughts and the images keep grabbing at her, wanting her attention, and eventually she shrugs, sighs, and lets her conscious mind follow the film that insists on playing out in her mind.

She is aware that someone in a blue and white striped nurse's uniform is standing next to her. The woman is asking her how she feels, and then, while she feels Thea's pulse, she adds that she fainted. Thea reflects that she has never fainted before; the nurse suggests that it was the injection, saying that it can sometimes have such an effect on some people.

Thea assumes that, obviously, she must be one of those people.

Now she can clearly remember the doctor and the injection. Then she remembers the man with the steel-rimmed glasses who had sat in the waiting room with her and how no one on the other side of the waiting room door has seen him since. She remembers that she had been standing in the middle of the Medical Centre and she was talking to someone - was it a secretary? - and she was about to ask something else when her head seemed to expand and fill the room, and everything went black.

Her mind swings back to the nurse hovering above her.

'You'll be all right in a moment or two,' the nurse says with professional conviction. 'Just drink this slowly.' She hands Thea a glass of something that looks like orange juice and Thea watches herself drink it obediently.

The Thea who is sitting in the waiting room really wants to ask the nurse about the man with the glasses, but the Thea who is in her head seems to have forgotten all about him. Though perhaps she has not forgotten: perhaps she simply realizes that the nurse is not going to know any more than the secretary, or if she knows she is probably not going to tell her anything.

She finishes the drink, hands the glass back to the nurse who is still standing next to her, swings her legs over the edge of the table, and stands up. Thea watches this other Thea, expecting her to be dizzy and unstable, but such is not the case, and she notes how she picks up her bag from the chair where someone has thoughtfully placed it, thanks the nurse, and asks for the way out of the clinic.

Thea frowns, wondering how the bag has become part of the image. She turns her head and notes that it is still sitting on the receptionist's desk. Was it simply wishful thinking, or is there a chance that she will get her bag back before she leaves the waiting room?

The nurse follows Thea out of the consulting room and points in the direction of the lift, not that far from room six.

Thea wonders why her shadow self does not go back and thank the secretary, but then she remembers that the secretary had mentioned something about finishing at nine and, according to the clock on the wall outside the consulting room, it is already half past. She sees herself smile at the nurse, and then, assuring her that she is okay, she walks towards the lift.

The following day, Aaron was back at work. Thea did not see him in the morning, and she was surprised to find him waiting for her in the courtyard when she turned up mid-morning for her break. Feelings of relief, excitement, and something else that she could not fully describe rushed around her body as she saw him, leaning against the wall, looking at the river. He looked tired and drawn, and Thea guessed that he had not slept for some time. He slid down the wall and sat on the warm red stones, indicating that she should do the same.

'I was so awfully worried,' she whispered. 'I'm not exactly sure why, but I was.'

He nodded and then looked at her with a wan smile. 'I really don't think that they have anything to go on,' he said, trying to comfort her. 'They think that they suspect something, but that's all.'

Thea wondered what it was they thought they suspected. The relationship that was barely a relationship? The meetings at the factory? The hidden bookcase? Everything?

She wondered briefly why there should even be a problem, but then, on further, deeper, more honest reflection, she had to admit that the Party would most probably have known she had been visiting Aaron. In fact, it was possible that they also knew about the meetings in the courtyard and on the bus. She was not sure about the bookcase - she hoped that it had managed to remain hidden. She admitted to herself what she had tried to avoid thinking about: the monitoring system used by Unitas was uncannily good, and there was no way to avoid it or even fool it. She thought back to when she left the house and how she had felt relieved, believing that no one had seen her. But had she stopped for a moment, she would have realized that she had been seen, and that Unitas knew that she had been visiting Aaron and how long she had been there.

Not that it should have been a problem. She was confused as she confronted the idea that she and Aaron could have done something considered to be outside of the regulations. No, it had nothing to do with their relationship, she decided, thinking back on their time together in Aaron's house. Perhaps the Party had dis-covered Aaron's store of books, or perhaps it was simply that it did not like some of his ideas and the way he and she were spending time together, discussing these ideas. Perhaps Unitas saw the two of them as a threat of some kind?

She wanted to cry out that she was absolutely not a threat. She had always complied with what the Party wanted. Admittedly, she was impulsive and had an active imagination, but she followed all the regulations; she had always fitted in; she had never really questioned what the Party did or did not do.

She became aware that Aaron was speaking to her, and she pulled her worried thoughts back from the Party's monitoring system and tried to concentrate on what he was saying.

He was telling her how he had been fetched the previous day by an official from the Department of Administration and Justice.

Thea's mind was racing: *so it was not the Department of Cohabitation and Population.*

The black hover had landed quietly outside the factory wall, and no one had seemed to suspect that anything was amiss when Aaron's supervisor had fetched him from his desk.

At the Department he had sat at a table on the twenty-second floor in a bleak, undecorated room, confronting three uniformed men who asked him questions about his work, his health, and his Party allegiance. From what he could gather, one of the men was a psychologist and the other two were Party officials. The man who was most probably a psychologist was thin and grey-haired with a nervous facial twitch, while his two colleagues were both decidedly corpulent and visibly more at ease. It quickly became obvious to Aaron that the three of them were working on a rotating system where one man asked a question, one man studied Aaron's reaction to the question, and the third man attempted to radiate a feeling of sympathy and understanding.

After exhausting the first three topics, they moved on to his food preferences, the type of music he listened to, and which football team he thought would win the premiership, each interrogator asking a question in turn while the remaining two either silently evaluated Aaron's answer or else concentrated on giving the illusion of being someone who both understood him and wanted to help him. As Aaron said to Thea: 'It was all completely and utterly bizarre.'

But all the time the three men had been watching him, calculating his reactions, taking notes on what he said and, most probably, on what he did not say. Halfway through the interview, they politely asked him if he preferred tea, coffee, or an energy drink, to which he had replied that he preferred coffee, and they had all taken a short break.

Thea wanted to ask if he had any idea why they had

fetched him and why they had interviewed him. She wanted to ask if they had mentioned her. Had they been following for him for days, weeks, months? Or perhaps the whole thing had been a mistake, and they had then admitted their blunder and apologized? Or perhaps it was a routine investigation and everyone at the factory would eventually be interviewed? There were so many things she wanted to ask, but she really did not know where to begin, so she said nothing.

Aaron may have understood her confusion; he may have even suspected what she wanted to ask. He said, 'I still have no idea why I was interviewed; I mean, they could have chosen anyone, and perhaps that was what it was all about - simply a random check. As I said, it was really very weird, almost as though they were trying to trick me. I really don't think that *what* I said was of any interest to them; it was *how* I said it.'

It was then that he pulled out his mini-PS and checked the time. It was already later than he had expected, and he said that they really should be getting back to work. They stood up, neither of them wanting to leave but knowing that they did not have a choice. As they left the courtyard, Aaron placed his hand on Thea's shoulder and told her not to worry.

He shook his head and said, 'They know everything about us - we know that - but there is nothing there that is of any importance. Not to them. Why they dragged me to the Department of Justice will probably remain a mystery, as far as I am concerned, but, hopefully, the experience will soon fade away, and everything will be normal again.'

Three days later Aaron did not turn up at work, and, although a month has passed since then, he has still not returned.

Thea is trying to remember what she has in her bag. It is not easy: she has a tendency to throw everything and anything into the bag and then forget that she has done so. She is almost certain that she has a woollen scarf - bright red with a complicated design of blue-red roses, purple flowers, and green leaves - a tube of face cream, an opened packet of hand wipes, a black comb (with two teeth missing), a half-eaten block of chocolate, the notebook with a red cover that she found in the antique shop, her PS, a pen, a small torch, and a book. The book, *The Buried Giant* by someone from long ago called Kazuo Ishiguro, belonged to Aaron. Strangely, it was not on the list of banned books, and Aaron had lent it to her one day in the courtyard, handing it to her while he talked about journeys and things we choose to remember and things we choose to forget. 'Obstacles need not be obstacles,' he had said, his hand still on the book. 'Things we may perceive as being negative and restrictive may in fact be our only salvation'. At the time she had thought his comments rather strange, but now, having read half the book, and with Aaron still missing, she felt that she was beginning to understand what he had been trying to tell her.

Unwilling to accept that Aaron was missing, she had concentrated on constructing a number of excuses for his absence: he was ill; he had been transferred; he was on a work trip to another sector. The excuses were all possible, and she hung on to them as a way of avoiding the thought that he may have been forcibly removed and would most probably not be coming back. She knew that people sometimes disappeared, but she had never given it a lot of thought; on the rare occasions when she fleetingly con- sidered such disappearances, she was certain that the Party knew what it was doing. Some people were decidedly a danger to the community, and it was for the good of the whole that they were made to disappear. Thea had always felt that it was important that everyone thought the same, or, if they did not think exactly the same about everything, that they could at least appreciate the importance of acting as a united whole. She had never really considered individual thought until she met Aaron, in the same way she had never considered what disappearance meant until Aaron disappeared.

She would have liked to have asked someone, but there was really no one to ask. When she had nonchalantly run the question past Jule, her friend had replied that people who disappeared were most likely executed or disposed of in some way - after all, none of them were seen again, so it made sense that they were probably clinically eliminated. When she looked quizzically at Thea and asked her why she was asking such a question, Thea had shrugged her shoulders and muttered something about the importance of knowing how the system worked, before changing the subject.

Looking back on the series of events that had led to Aaron's disappearance, Thea believes that it must have been all her fault. Had she not agreed to the meetings with Aaron at the factory; had she not encouraged him; and, most importantly, had she not made the impulsive decision to follow him home, he would most probably still be working at the factory. He would be safely in his office, checking workflows and orders and all the other things he did, and she would not be worrying about where he was or, more importantly, *if* he was.

Aaron's disappearance has impacted Thea in many ways: not only is she extremely worried, with a dense and overpowering sense of guilt, she has also become acutely aware of the interrelation between things and events. This awareness has burst upon her, somewhat like a thundery shower on an otherwise warm, sunny summer's day. She has always known that there is an inter-connectedness between things - at least, she thinks she has - but it has never been something to which she has given very much thought.

Now she cannot stop thinking about how each situation, each conversation, and each meeting are all linked, pushing the people involved in different directions, collecting new people while discarding others. Just one small change to a single one of these situations can create a completely different web of events with completely different people and completely different outcomes.

If only she had not stayed on the bus.

Thea tries to push her thoughts away from Aaron, and she studies the room instead. She quite likes the yellow walls, and she feels that dark grey works well on the doors and even on the receptionist's chair; however, ignoring the colour scheme, she feels that there are a number of things that probably need to be rectified. To start with, the chairs should not be plastic; they should be proper chairs and padded; moreover, arranging them in two lines looking at the exit door is both bad design and bad psychology. Thea decides that, if she were in charge, she would move them closer to the side walls, and she would arrange them in a more haphazard, casual fashion. Having the chairs more to the side would give everyone a better view of the room, the two doors, and the receptionist.

She would definitely hang some paintings on the very bare walls and she would install a water dispenser and also a coffee/tea machine. The phrase: *Bring nothing with you* would be removed from the letter, and people would be encouraged to use their personal screens.

As she thinks more about how the room could be redecorated, she adds a large screen to the front wall, next to the exit door, where information regarding waiting times could be displayed every fifteen minutes or so. There could also be messages, and apologies, concerning delays or changes to the timetable.

And, most importantly, she would employ a more pleasant receptionist.

There is a noise in the corridor behind her; it sounds like some kind of commotion, and Thea turns around, wondering what might be going on. The receptionist is not moving, so Thea assumes that it is nothing to worry about.

But the noise continues - it sounds like a couple of people having an argument - and Thea begins to feel ill at ease and even agitated. She notices that most people are now turning to look at the receptionist, waiting to see what she is going to do.

Initially, the receptionist does nothing. She looks as though she is trying to pretend that she has not heard the noise. Then there is a knocking at the door, followed by a louder, more demonstrative knocking, and it irritates Thea to see the receptionist still sitting at her desk, pretending not to have heard anything. In another situation, with another receptionist, Thea may even have got up and opened the door herself; however, she does not feel that that would be her best decision in the present situation.

Eventually, the receptionist stands up, at the same time as a security guard enters the waiting room. He is holding on to a large, rather dishevelled, man and the two of them make their way across the back of the room to the receptionist's desk. Although Thea would like to know what has been going on and why the security guard is now in the waiting room, she does not feel that she should continue watching, and she turns back to look at the long stretch of wall and the exit door.

She can hear the security guard talking with the receptionist, but their speech is somewhat muted and eventually she loses interest. Obviously, it must all be somehow work-related, and it is most probably something that only concerns the receptionist and the security guard, and possibly the rather dejected-looking man.

The main thing is that the altercation or disturbance or whatever it was has been brought to an end. Thea is vaguely interested, but she is already back in her own thoughts.

A few minutes later, a woman sitting in the front row is called to the exit door. She has barely disappeared through the door before the receptionist calls out another number. The thought runs through Thea's head that the receptionist is probably trying to get rid of everyone as quickly as possible.

There is a pause. No one gets up. Thea does a quick survey of the room and wonders why no one has gone to the door.

The receptionist calls out impatiently, '3325-678 to the door immediately.'

Thea starts, this time hearing the number in all its familiarity. She stands up, wondering why she did not recognize it the first time but delighted that the long wait is now over; she has, after all, been sitting in the waiting room for the best part of two hours. She desperately needs to talk to someone who is both understanding and sympathetic, and she is hoping that someone will be waiting for her on the other side of the door - a someone who might want to help her.

At the same time, two more security guards enter the waiting room and Thea is vaguely aware that they are talking with the first guard.

She is about to walk towards the door when she remembers the film that has been playing backwards and forwards in her head. She remembers how, in those images, she had her bag, the bag that is still sitting on the receptionist's desk. Were the images trying to tell her something? Is she supposed to have her bag when she leaves the waiting room? She is not sure, but more than anything she wants her bag, and she is almost certain that she will not see it again if she leaves it where it is sitting.

Aware that the receptionist now has her attention tied to the three guards and the man about to disappear through the door at the front of the room, Thea takes a deep breath, moves behind the line of chairs, walks quickly across the room, and sweeps up her bag from the receptionist's desk.

The woman, taken by surprise, removes her eyes from the door, drops her knitting, and lunges out at the bag, but she is just a fraction too slow and too late.

With the bag clenched in her arms, Thea runs towards

the door at the front of the room. The remaining three people in the room are shaken back into life after hours of inertia, their heads turned, their eyes moving from the girl in the green coat to the receptionist.

The receptionist has noisily pushed back her chair and is already on her feet. She is angry: no one treats her with such a blatant lack of respect. It has never happened before and it will certainly not happen now.

She rushes across the room, waving her arms and screaming, 'Stop! I said *stop*. Stay right where you are! You may not—'

But it is too late. Thea opens the door and steps out of the room.

The door slams shut behind her.

THE RECEPTIONIST

7891-447 has disappeared through the door and the receptionist sits at her desk, carefully counting the stitches on her knitting needle. She becomes distracted, loses count, and has to start all over again. While she is counting, she is thinking that there was something about 7891-447 that she did not like, or was it simply that he may have stirred up memories she did not want to confront? She is not sure, and she continues to ponder as she finishes her counting, places the knitting on the desk, and looks out over the people in the room. She discovered a long time ago that she does not particularly like people; in fact, she would have to admit that there is probably no one with whom she feels that she has the slightest connection - close or otherwise. The only reason that she is sitting in the waiting room, in charge of this group of disparate people, is because of her apparent lack of empathy. 'We can't possibly have someone who might want to *connect,*' they had said, and then they had all suddenly thought of her - the person who never seems to connect with anyone.

The receptionist - or 8733-110, which is how she has thought of herself for just on two decades - *did* have a name once upon a time, but she likes to pretend that she has completely forgotten it. When the Party insisted that all citizens who were around before the Change must forget their names, or at least appear to forget them, the receptionist did as she was asked: she likes to be seen as complying with whatever the Party demands of her. If she is totally honest, she has to admit that she does still remember her name; she was, after all, already in her thirties when the Change finally took place, and it is not easy to forget something that has been an important part of your life for more than three decades. But, if anyone should ask her what her original name was (a question that no one in their right mind would be willing to ask of anyone), she would confidently answer that she has absolutely no idea.

She turns her head and looks at the clock, and, as she does so, she wonders for the hundredth time whose idea it was to put the clock on the wall behind her desk; it should have been placed on the front wall. She is feeling extremely irritated: according to her roster, she was supposed to have ended her shift a few minutes ago, but there are still people in the waiting room, and she cannot leave until they have all passed through the door at the front of the room. If the timetable functioned as it was supposed to, she would now be packing up her PS and her knitting and getting ready to leave both the waiting room and the building. It is already well past seven-thirty and she does not have to remind herself that she has been on duty since midday. The seven people remaining in the waiting room still have to be processed, so she tries to resign herself to the fact that her shift will not end until they have all passed through the door. If it had been left up to the receptionist, she would have bundled the lot of them through the door together, but that is not the way Administration wants things done. The receptionist and the people in Administration have some very different ideas about how things should be run, but they have all silently decided to agree to disagree; it is easier that way - the receptionist needs the work and the feeling of importance that goes with it, while Administration needs what they feel is her lack of empathy. A 'win-win' situation for everyone involved, the receptionist thinks.

She is not what anyone would call attractive. Well into her fifties, of average height and extremely thin, she does not belong to the 'fit and slim' image to which most women aspire; instead, she can only be described as unpleasantly angular. Her hair is short, grey, and wiry and her nails are lacquered with bright red varnish - the only extravagance she allows herself.

Extravagance is a concept that took on a very negative connotation after Unitas came to power. Prior to the change of power, commercialism and extravagance had been two of the things holding the society together. 'Spend, purchase. Splurge!' the politicians had urged their constituents, painting a verbal picture of money swirling through the community and settling in the pockets of the many, and not, as a number of sceptics argued, only in the pockets of the few. When, after the Change, excessive squandering was labelled both irresponsible and sinful - although, in a secular society such as Unitas, it was difficult to know whom or what was being sinned against - people very quickly learnt to restrain their spending. There was, after all, a limited selection of things to purchase - commercialism had been overtaken by renunciation.

She sits at her desk, her shiny black PS in front of her. She is, however, not absorbing any of the words that flash past on the screen, as her thoughts keep reverting to 7891-447, the man who had been sitting in the back row. There had been something about him that had irritated or, at the very least, upset her: was it the fact that he was overly anxious - she normally has very little time for distressed people - or was it simply something about the way he looked? She is not sure, but with his tall build and dark hair and glasses he reminded her of someone she knew a long while ago. Someone she believed she had forgotten.

Her thoughts baulk a little, make a sharp turn, and move to the girl with the bag. What was her number? She flicks through the papers in front of her and, while holding some papers in her left hand, pulls out a paper from the middle of the pile. Yes, that was it: 3325-678. A really stuck-up piece of bad news. She looks over to where the girl is sitting and purses her lips. Who does she think she is, demanding to keep her confounded, awful bag? The receptionist returns the paper to the pile and places the other papers neatly on top. She hopes that 3325-678 will get her rightful comeuppance on the other side of the door.

She resents the fact that she has already been contacted by one of the officials from beyond the waiting room. Administration had been immensely annoyed and irritated by the woman who had caused all the fuss earlier. The bureaucrat who contacted her had been emphatic: such displays of emotion simply cannot be tolerated; they waste everyone's time and they are bad for the morale of the other people in the room. Before ending the conversation (which had been translated into 16-point bold text on her PS), the official had reminded her tersely that it is also of utmost importance to keep to the time schedule.

Of course *she* knows it is important to keep to the schedule, but obviously other people are not that particular. She turns her head and looks at the clock, yet again; the hands do not seem to have moved since she last looked. Clocks, especially analogue clocks, more or less disappeared years ago, as time, digitally formatted, could be accessed on any personal screen with the lightest of taps. Clocks, like the one on the waiting room wall, are now only kept as curiosities from a time long past. The receptionist has never completely understood why Administration would have decided to hang an analogue clock in the waiting room: she wonders if it was an attempt to give people a chance to watch the passing of time. She thinks about this possibility for a minute but then decides that if this was how Administration thought then it makes no sense whatsoever, given that the clock is on the wall behind her desk and behind all the people in the waiting room. Obviously, there must have been another, more obscure, reason.

Her thoughts drift away from the clock and begin to move around the word *schedule*, and she asks herself what she is supposed to do when an out-of-control woman goes to pieces. It has happened a few times in the past, and each and every time Administration has chosen to see such a breach of normal waiting-room behaviour as her fault. Even this time, Administration, as always, was adamant: it is obvious that *she* must have done something that instigated the whole event, or perhaps she did not do something that she should have done. Still fuming over the conversation, she decides that all Administration bureaucrats should spend a few days in the waiting room and then perhaps they would have a different understanding of things like time wasting and schedules and general morale. She cannot be expected to be responsible for people going to pieces; it amazes her at times that there are not more people who lose control.

The image of the overly large woman in the burgundy dress fills her mind, and she can feel her anger swelling within her. Whenever she has had to deal with hysterical clients she has always found it more annoying than upsetting, especially when she realizes that she will be blamed for it happening at all.

Then, for no obvious reason, she finds herself once again thinking of the tall man with the black hair and steel-rimmed glasses, not the one in the waiting room but the other one, the one she knew all those years ago. She gropes around in her memory and she remembers that he was called Walter - she does not know his number; people still had names when she knew Walter - and he was studying at the university. Law? Political Science? She is no longer certain. What she can remember is that she was eighteen or nineteen, and he was a few years older. She can also remember that she used to wear her fair hair pulled back in a ponytail, believing that it suited her, and she recalls that she was fully convinced that she was deeply and passionately in love.

Even back then, no one would have called her beautiful; most people, if asked, would have possibly said that she was exceedingly plain. Her most impressive feature, her skin, was smooth, on the olive side of white and completely without any form of blemish, but that was all. Her lips were thin and her eyes small, and even then, all those years ago, she was what many would have called 'painfully thin'. She had not been able to believe that someone like Walter would look at her twice, but for some unknown reason he did.

Thinking about Walter now makes her feel as though she has entered a time machine that has propelled her backwards, to a moment, so far back in the past, that it is debatable if it even exists any longer, or whether it ever existed in the first place. She does not think of herself as that person any longer - the-person-who-she-once-was - nor does she normally think of Walter.

She reflects that things had unfortunately not worked out the way she had imagined or hoped they would.

Her work in the waiting room on floor thirty-six of Building C is not particularly demanding: it is simply a matter of collecting the letters handed to her by the clients, noting numbers, which she then orders into a schedule, and not showing any empathy. This last requirement is probably the most important, and it is something with which she has no problem, but she occasionally has a feeling that it was not always so: there was a time, many years ago, when she feels - she can no longer remember for sure - that she may have found it relatively easy to empathize with other people.

When she first met Walter, she, like so many other people, had only just become aware of Unitas. There had been a few articles in the online newspapers - newspapers as physical entities had completely disappeared years previously - and a number of online programmes where various top-ranking people from within the Party were questioned in regard to policy and direction. No one could argue against the fact that the Party was still in its infancy, and because of this everyone assumed that it did not pose any kind of threat to the status quo. But after having survived a couple of decades in the womb of clandestine meetings and debate, it was slowly emerging as a small player on the political scene. While most of the media were initially hesitant or not at all interested, there were a couple of journalists who were already able to see a little further than their colleagues: they painted verbal pictures of a society that was no longer democratic, and they asked their readers to think about the value of personal freedom and how important it was to be able to retain a high standard of living and an above-par quality of life.

The majority of people decided that the journalists were being alarmists for no good reason, while the three major political parties, not quite as cerebral as the two journalists, made it clear, somewhat derisively, that although Unitas may be presenting itself as a temporary annoyance, it was most unlikely that it would ever be a contender for government.

However, among the ordinary people there was a growing number who believed that the idea of putting the whole before the individual could possibly be advantageous for a disintegrating society, even though there were still many who were not convinced. Some of those who were sceptical based their opposition on stories of twentieth-century communism they had heard related or which they had stumbled over when researching topics as disparate as state-versus-private ownership, equality, competition, and even labour camps. But for most people the idea of Unitas was, in many ways, simply a pleasant diversion from the normal run of political games as played by the three major parties, and it gave rise to numerous dinner-table discussions - discussions that lacked any form of gravity or importance and where people could safely be either for or against or indecisively somewhere in the middle.

By the time she met Walter, the person who would one day become the receptionist was already tentatively moving beyond the dinner table in a somewhat definite direction and had, on one occasion, attended a local Unitas party meeting in a cold, bleak community hall. She was curious, but she was still not overly interested in getting involved. She had too many other things with which to fill her mind: her university studies, and now Walter, among them.

When Building C was not even a minute fleck in anyone's mind, and when the idea of an unfeeling receptionist directing people to uncomfortable chairs in a claustrophobic waiting room was still hidden somewhere on a planet in a parallel universe, she would, on occasion, read articles or watch programmes that sought to present and clarify the ideas and policies of Unitas. Growing up, she had never been particularly interested in politics - she assumed that whatever Party her parents voted for was most probably the best, not because she had done any research into policies or track records but because she felt that all political Parties were basically the same. As far as she could judge, they all had their own agendas that rarely had anything to do with the people they were governing or whom they hoped to govern. In the years before her curiosity got the better of her, and before she began investigating Unitas, it made sense to her to follow in her parents' footsteps - there were too many other things that were far more important than politics.

But there was something unique about Unitas that caught her attention: she was not sure whether it was the core policy of putting the whole before the individual or whether it was the fact that Unitas was the political under-dog. In the derision meted out towards the newcomer by the other parties it is possible that she may have vaguely recognized elements of her own situation. She was never quite sure what it was that grabbed hold of her and directed her to the meeting in the draughty community hall, but after that meeting she occasionally began to attend the irregular information talks that Unitas held on the university campus. She was still not completely converted, so she kept herself quietly on the edge, listening, considering, weighing up the pluses and minuses. Sometimes Walter would join her, but he was wary of the fundamental premise of the Party: the idea that the individual and individual freedom should be sacrificed for the whole.

It was the one point on which they could not see eye to eye, but she never expected it to be a hurdle: she did not see politics as being a big thing in their lives. They had their studies and each other; nothing else was particularly important.

Then one day she looked around and realized that Walter was no longer part of her life.

The receptionist calls out another number, and a somewhat obese man in an ill-fitting grey suit, sitting in the front row of chairs, gets heavily to his feet and trundles slowly to the door. She waits until he disappears, and then she drops the paper in the bin and looks out over the room.

As far as she is concerned, it is a small, compact room that could have benefited from the addition of at least one window; she finds it wearying to sit in such an enclosed space, day after day, without having any contact with the outside. She is not sure that it can be healthy, spending so much time in artificial light, apart from which she never has the slightest idea as to whether the sun is shining or whether it is raining. Although she is not especially particular about being at one with the natural world, she feels that a window through which she could see sky and clouds, and possibly even other buildings, would most likely boost her overall mood. Looking at white walls, day in and day out, month in and month out, is not something that most people would sign up for voluntarily. Her thoughts move to skewed images of old-fashioned mental hospitals from a time now well and truly allocated to the past, and, for a moment, she feels a twinge of what can only be described as insight or perhaps even recognition. Her perception, however, is more sub-conscious than conscious, and after flickering to life very quickly disappears into the regulated patterns of her mind.

She looks across the heads of the people in front of her, wondering what their thoughts might be and how they might relate to the room. Do they, like she, miss not having a window or even several windows? Do they feel constricted, even claustrophobic, just like she does? Are they also frustrated by a clock that has been placed in the wrong place on the wrong wall? Do they spend all their time in the waiting room, wondering what is on the other side of the exit door?

Not that it really concerns her one way or the other, but she feels that it would be interesting to know what others think of the room. If she has learnt anything in life, she has learnt that no one sees or experiences anything exactly the same way as anyone else. Although she does not want to think about Walter, she recalls how they often argued about what they had seen, and what they had done and what they then remembered.

She picks up her black ballpoint pen and runs a finger over the gold trim - it is one of her very few, and therefore treasured, possessions. It was given to her after ten years of service. She suspects that the idea of presenting her with a pen may have been tongue-in-cheek - no one uses pens any longer. Perhaps someone was trying to make a point - because she is different, because she manages to rile some people, because she still has a foot in a time that is not Unitas. Then she wonders briefly if it may have also had something to do with a collective sense of guilt regarding the lack of windows. A small flicker of a smile, almost contemptuous, flickers across her face before disappearing.

Pens, like clocks, are obsolete - collectors' items at best. With all communication now managed via the PS, people no longer need to write - in fact, not many people *can* write. There are still a few people, like the receptionist, who appreciate the feel of the slender utensil between their fingers and who occasionally like being able to make their own marks on paper, not simply electronic marks on a screen. Secretly, the receptionist relishes the insignificant, but, for her important, feeling of superiority that comes with being able to use a pen, even though she now only uses it to write numbers on the small pieces of paper. She knows that she is the only receptionist who uses pen and paper, and she knows that it is completely unnecessary - the PS contains all information regarding both the clients and their schedules - but the knowledge that she has her own way of doing things simply strengthens her belief that she is different to, and perhaps a little more accomplished than, the other receptionists.

Returning the pen to its place on the white melamine surface of her very simple desk, she leans back in her black leather chair. She has had the chair for more than five years - it had taken a lot of negotiating and even grovelling, but she feels that it was worth it. At least now she can feel comfortable while she is looking at the white walls.

When the last person has finally passed through the white panelled door at the back of the room, she will carefully pack her knitting, her pen, her communications device, and her PS into her large black bag and tidy the desk, not that there is much to tidy. She will collect the blank paper into a neat pile and dust the surface. Then, when the desk has been returned to pristine order and cleanliness, she will take a brisk walk along the lines of chairs, straightening them and moving them back into two ordered rows, before finally waving her wrist over the light plate and leaving the room.

Her unit is close by, so she will not have to take a bus after she exits Building C, and she will walk the five hundred or so metres, keeping close to the buildings. If it is a pleasant evening, she will walk slowly, enjoying the fresh air and the fact that she is finally outside even though it will doubtlessly already be dark. It is more than likely that she will meet a few people, people like herself who finish late and others who are on their way to late-night shifts, but when she meets anyone, she will keep her head down and walk straight ahead, avoiding eye contact. At her building – a grey and white high-rise with a textured façade - she will raise her wrist to the pad near the front door, and she will then wait for the heavy door to swing open so that she can step inside. There will probably be a few people in the foyer or in the lift, and she will nod to them politely as one does when one shares a building, a foyer, and a lift. It is even possible that she may recognize one or two of them.

On the fifth floor she will depart the lift and, using her bracelet a second time, will open the door to her unit, which is directly across the corridor from the lift. It will be quiet inside, and there will perhaps be a vague smell of staleness or simply strands of that elusive smell associated with a closed-up space - no one will have been there since morning. She will activate the lights and the air conditioning and place her bag on the slate-topped table in the small entrance hall. She will then walk through to the rectangular living room. Walking to the window overlooking a stretch of green between her building and the next, she will push some buttons on a console governing the amount of light coming in through the window. The window will immediately turn dark and opaque and the light in the room will seem brighter and warmer.

In the small but well-equipped kitchen, she will heat some water for tea while she takes a meal packet from the stainless-steel cupboard and places it in the RF for instant heating. She may even turn on her PS, selecting a programme with people talking or perhaps even a concert, hoping, subconsciously, to cut through the silence and the sense of isolation.

The receptionist's thoughts about what she will most likely do after she leaves Building C have suddenly swirled into one of a myriad black holes, and she is once again thinking of Walter. She reflects briefly that it is strange that she has already thought of him so many times in one day; she has not seen him for more than twenty years, and during all that time she does not believe that she has thought of him once. Or perhaps she has? She is no longer completely sure. All she knows with complete certainty is that she has no idea where he is now, or what he is doing or even what he looks like. He could have put on weight and turned grey; he may not even wear glasses any longer - many people have discarded them as old-fashioned. She wonders whether he married and whether he may have had children before everything changed. When she thinks about children, she also thinks of the present system where children are moved through homes as though on some kind of conveyor belt, and she forces her thoughts in another direction. As her thoughts are slipping away from children's homes and the reorganization of the concept of family, she thinks how, on the past side of her present, she had always believed that she and Walter would have gone through life together.

Now that he is foremost in her mind, she remembers

how he had excused himself from a Giles Bancroft concert for which they had been extremely lucky to get tickets - she had queued for more than six hours - and how, only a week later, he had suddenly told her that he would have to miss a planned weekend trip to the mountains. They had both been very excited about the mountain trip; it was something that they had been talking about for several months, so she found it strange that he would cancel almost at the last minute. He had been evasive, but when she insisted on an explanation he said that his parents had arranged a family event and that they expected him to attend.

She had reluctantly accepted his excuses, telling herself that things sometimes happen over which neither she nor anyone have any control, and she did not really start to worry until he began to miss their mid-morning rendezvous. These meetings, usually at one of the several coffee shops or on one of the grassed areas that spread out between the university buildings, reinforced, for her at least, the feeling that they had a special connection, and that they belonged to each other. She could accept that they were not able to meet every day - there were so many things that managed to elbow themselves to the front of the queue - but each day he had a new excuse: he had to finish an essay; he had an unexpected tutorial; he was coming down with the 'flu; his sister needed help moving into a new flat, buying kitchenware, washing the cat... and then the excuses stopped altogether. She tried phoning him, but when she called she always got his answering machine or else the call simply rang out. Something inside of her began to swell up into an enormous question mark; in fact, it was so big, it was the only thing of which she was aware. Was there a logical reason for his silence, was it simply bad luck, or was it something else entirely?

The relationship stopped being a relationship. It was like writing on sand being washed over by waves - it simply ceased to be. She was never exactly certain when it happened, but she knew that it was somewhere in between all the excuses and all the broken appointments. She was never certain if it had something to do with her political opinions or if there was someone else. In the end, it really did not matter.

For the girl who would one day become the receptionist, all the question marks suddenly received an answer: he had left her, and slowly the question marks began evaporating, one by one. Even the question as to why he had done it disappeared with all the others. She had never understood why Walter had been attracted to her in the first place; she had always told herself that she never really deserved someone like Walter.

Once it had become apparent that he had definitely cast her aside, she subconsciously tried to avoid him. Then, some months later, their paths crossed, and, realizing that she could not just stand there speechless and that she would have to say something, she said that she missed him and that she was trying to understand. She would have liked to have screamed at him, or said something sarcastic, or even burst into tears, but although there were lots of snide comments that came easily to her mind, she knew that she was not an openly emotional person, and it was most unlikely that she would shed any tears irrespective how she felt on the inside.

He had stood with one foot on the path, and the other on the newly mowed grass, his backpack hanging from one shoulder. He had looked surprised, uncomfortable, and apologetic all at once, and she had even noticed a slight red flush rising from his neck and heading for his hairline.

For a moment she thought that he may have wanted to say something, but she interrupted him before he could harness the words into a sentence. The fleeing question marks had left her feeling empty and worthless, but she could not afford for him to realize how she really felt.

'Have a great life, Walter', she said. 'It was wonderful.' She was going to add 'while it lasted', but the feelings of emptiness and despair were threatening to choke her, so she waved her hand in the air as though she was not sure whether she would shake his hand, hug him, or slap him across the face, and, turning quickly, disappeared into the crowd of people thronging outside the lecture hall.

When she was still a child, long before she came in contact with Walter and Unitas and the waiting room, she wore her hair in two spindly light-coloured plaits that were simply a reiteration of her two skinny arms and two skinny legs. She was not what anyone would have called ugly, but, on the other hand, she was not pretty. At school she was always on the fringe of the group - the girl who was accepted only when there were too few children to play a certain game or when it was to the group's advantage to excel at a school project. The pretty, self-confident girls with their newest electronic devices and their large following of social-media admirers formed the hub of the group, each one vying with the others to be at the very centre.

She may not have been particularly good-looking, but she was intelligent, and she soon learnt to use this to her advantage. Even at home, where she lived with her parents and, for a short period, a brother who was ten years her senior, she became adept at manipulating situations to her own advantage. Despite her lack of any photogenic superiority or social-media followers, she steadfastly set herself goals and achieved them; that is, until Walter suddenly left her.

Her device blinks, and she picks up the next paper and reads off the number. The woman who is dressed all in black stands up, turns, and looks directly at her for a few seconds before walking quickly to the door. The look is both penetrating and cold. The receptionist is somewhat taken aback: she is not sure what the look is supposed to convey, so she tries to pretend that it never happened. Could it be possible that the woman is blaming her for something? For waiting so long? For having to walk through the door? For what may or may not be on the other side of the door? She is not sure. While trying to remove the look from her mind, she checks the progress of her knitting and then begins a new row.

One of the many problems with being a receptionist is that, without volunteering, one becomes the person whom everyone likes to blame. She knows that she has often been blamed for the long waiting time, and she is quite sure that there are many people who, even if they are relatively understanding about the waiting time, undoubtedly start blaming her once they pass through the door.

She moves her gaze to the back of Thea's head and thinks to herself that 3325- (she cannot recall the rest of the number) is more than possibly one of these people; in all likelihood, she is sitting there, blaming her for absolutely everything. In fact, she is probably thinking of nothing else.

The understanding that each and every person in the room is like a container filled with unrelated thoughts, emotions, and even dreams is not something new for the receptionist. She has often looked out over the sundry collection of people in front of her, wondering at the different apprehensions, interpretations, and reflections that might be passing through their minds. She doubts that the thoughts are at all ordered, in all likelihood they are intersected by fears and question marks - none of the people in the waiting room really knows why they are there, and it is the *not knowing* that is feeding the fear and giving rise to the question marks.

Though some think they know.

The receptionist's eyes travel to the bag sitting on her desk, and she sighs. Of course, the bag will have to be processed: there is always more work when people bring along personal effects. She cannot understand why they do it: surely the letter is clear enough: '*bring nothing with you*', it says. The receptionist moves her eyes back to Thea, and, for a brief instant, in spite of everything she is and has become, together with her supposed lack of either sympathy or empathy, she feels suddenly and strangely moved by the image of the rope of thick brown hair against the green coat.

There are only five people left in the waiting room. The receptionist continues knitting; she has always found that knitting relaxes her. She used to knit all those years ago when she first met Walter, and she remembers that she knitted him a couple of jumpers - one was brown with a complicated cable pattern - doubtlessly long since discarded. She used to believe that keeping her hands busy prevented her from having to think about other things, but she is no longer so certain. Now she wonders if the repetitive action could be a kind of physical mantra that simply takes the edge off all those things that may be worrying her - wrapping them in cotton wool in other words. She smiles at the image and begins a new row.

Initially she had found it difficult to fully grasp that Walter had left her, despite the fact that she had always been curious as to why he would have been interested in her in the first place. Once she had assimilated the shock of him wanting to be with her, she had decided that physical appearances were probably not an important part of their relationship. They were obviously attracted to each other because of other, deeper, things. By the time he walked out on her, they had been seeing each other regularly for more than two years. She had already begun to imagine the shape their life together would take; she no longer even bothered to envisage a future without him – as far as she was concerned, even if they were not exactly following the same path, they were still moving in the same direction.

The instant she saw all his excuses for what they were - a letter, or many letters, of resignation - her past life finished and her new life commenced. At that precise moment she had no idea what shape her new life would take; all she knew was that Walter was not going to be part of it, and that they were neither moving along the same path nor in the same direction.

The evening grinds on, interminable second by interminable second. At times she wonders if perhaps the clock may have stopped, and then she wonders what would happen if time itself, not just the recorder of time passing, should stop. Would everything stop, disintegrate, explode, implode? She is not sure, but the thought is both captivating and extremely worrying.

If time stopped, would she be where she is now, or would she be somewhere else? Or would she be every-where at the same time? The world would stop spinning, the wind would stop blowing, and the waves on all the oceans would stop moving. She tries to imagine an ocean with no movement and towns and cities full of motionless people. She had heard a theory that a train, travelling at the speed of light, would in effect be stopping time, but she had never been able to get her head around the physics. She finds the image of a motionless, timeless world or train too much to contemplate, and she decides that the clock has not stopped and that the possibility of time stopping is inconceivable.

Some days, the waiting room is completely empty before seven-thirty and the receptionist is free to leave; other days she does not get away before eight or, at times, eight-thirty or even nine o'clock. She has never been able to work out what the problem is: Administration knows how many people are coming through on any particular day; surely they should be able to have everyone processed before seven-thirty?

When the fact that Walter was not going to be part of her future finally struck her with a force that she later equated with how she imagined it would feel to be hit by a ten-tonne truck, she felt as though she had been shipwrecked a long way from shore. She had been building up an imaginary future with Walter at its centre, and when it all fell apart she found that she had nothing to hold on to. Or, at least, she thought that that was the case, but as she desperately hunted through the debris for something, anything, that might support her, she found

Unitas. She remembered the few meetings and talks she had attended and the ideas that she had found somewhat interesting, and she grabbed on to the plank that was Unitas and floated to the shore.

Elections were held later that year and as Unitas stormed to victory she felt relieved that she had grabbed the right plank: she had no idea where she was headed, but wherever it was, there were lots of other people headed in the same direction.

She is still thinking about the time it takes to process a waiting room filled with people; she is certain that the whole operation could easily be reorganized and streamlined, but no one asks for her opinion. Not any more. In the beginning, when everything was new and exciting - it was a bit like stepping on to an uninhabited planet - everyone listened to everyone else. The pivotal idea of putting the whole before the individual was fixed and could not be changed, but there was so much around that idea that needed to be discussed and put into operation. For a while, she worked for one of the ministers, then the years passed, and new people replaced those who had been in office from the beginning. The newer, younger people were often focused on career possibilities, and she was gently pushed to one side as the central idea mutated and expanded. Eventually, someone in the Sector where she was living decided that she would be perfect as receptionist on floor thirty-six of Building C. She often wondered if the receptionists on floor thirty-six of Building C in all the many sectors around the country were just like she was or if they were different. It really did not matter; it was unlikely that she would ever meet any of them.

The receptionist's attention is caught by a disturbance beyond the waiting room. The noise is coming from further down the corridor, and it sounds like a commotion or a confrontation of some kind. A couple of people in the waiting room turn around, wondering, like the receptionist, what might be going on.

She is uncomfortably aware of the annoying, jarring sounds while she keeps her eyes on the five people sitting in front of her. She does not like disturbances of any kind, and this one is upsetting her. Moreover, it does not make a lot of sense: the only people allowed on floor thirty-six are the people who have been called to the waiting room. The lift does not stop there for anyone else. Whoever is in the corridor must have got past lift security somehow, but she cannot work out how that would be possible.

As a child she lived in a tired block of flats between a takeaway on one side and a relatively new concrete high-rise on the other, and disturbance in its many different guises was an accepted part of life. Sometimes, though, it stopped being simply a word that she could shy away from and became a reality that felt too close and too confronting, and, when this happened, and often while blue lights rotated through the white and red and yellow lights patterning her window, she would bury herself under the bedclothes and block her ears. In spite of her precautions, the discordant sounds always seemed to find their way under the blankets and between the fingers pressed tightly against her ears even while she was telling herself that everything was all right and that there was nothing to fear.

Although she still does not like people losing control and shouting and being physically abusive, sitting in the waiting room all these years later she knows that she is unable to hide under blankets or even cover her ears.

Part of her mind lingers around the block of flats where she grew up, while another part tries to work out how unauthorized people have been able to access floor thirty-six. She is also wondering if it is something to which she should attend.

She scrolls through her PS to see if there is anyone else on her list for the day, but everyone is already in the waiting room, and she is hoping that they will be processed as soon as possible, and she will then be able to go home.

The commotion is becoming very loud, and she is

aware of a sense of unease moving through the waiting room. Obviously, the very few people left in the waiting room expect her to do something; perhaps someone has already been hurt or is in the process of being hurt.

As she considers this last possibility, her mind stops processing so many thoughts simultaneously, and she concentrates on what she should or should not be doing, and how she should or should not be doing it. The guidelines are very clear: the person on duty in the waiting room should not, under any circumstance, leave the room. But she would not have to leave the room, or would she?

Since the episode with the hysterical woman and the dressing-down she received from the Administration official, she is feeling extremely anxious and stressed. She tries to concentrate on her knitting, wrapping the wool around the needle and pulling the new stitch through the old one. Her mind, however, will not leave her in peace; she wonders, yet again, if she should be doing something—

A chill runs through her body as she realizes that if she *should* be doing something and is not doing anything then she will have to have a good explanation for sitting behind her desk while someone may be dying in the corridor beyond the door. She is not sure if Administration will accept her excuse that she was simply adhering to the guidelines. She wonders if her day can get any worse. She tries to steer her thoughts away from things over which she feels she has no control and knits a few more stitches.

The noise from the corridor has not subsided; in fact, it has become louder and, if possible, more aggressive. She tells herself that she has to do something, but she is not sure what. She picks up her communication device and presses the button for security. She waits for several seconds, and when nothing happens, she pushes it again. Security is supposed to be on the job 24/7. This is obviously a problem for security; it has nothing to do with a receptionist in a waiting room.

While she is wondering about her next step, her finger still poised above the security button, the device flashes with the message that she can send through the next client. She is grateful to be brought back to her own reality, even if only temporarily, and she tries to persuade herself that the noise in the corridor is outside her area of concern. It is something that security should be monitoring, and if they cannot be contacted then it can hardly be seen as her fault. She pushes the device to one side, and she calls out the next number.

The fracas has moved along the corridor and sounds as though it is now right outside the door to the waiting room. There is a knock at the door. She starts. No one ever knocks at the door; people simply open it and enter. There is a sign on the door that clearly states that it is a waiting room; why would anyone knock on the door to a waiting room? Unless, of course, it is connected to the noise in the corridor. Perhaps it really *is* an emergency, and perhaps someone needs help. She gazes around the room, wondering if anyone else has heard the knock. It comes again, and the four people remaining in the room all turn their heads.

Normally self-reliant and superficially independent, she has been thrown into a situation where she is not sure what to do next. This is a strange experience for the receptionist, and she tries to take control again by confining her thought processes. She forces herself to concentrate on her knitting and tries to give the appearance that there is no knock, or if there is that she has not heard it. The regulations say that that her concentration must never move from the people in the waiting room: things beyond the waiting room have absolutely nothing to do with her. There are a lot of things about Administration that she finds frustrating and out of sync with the society it is attempting to govern, but this is hardly the time or the place to be reflecting on such complications.

The noise in the corridor has reached a crescendo, and the remaining people again turn and look at her. Curiously. Expectantly. She punches in the code to the security officer on duty, but there is still no answer. She begins to stand up slowly, thinking that it cannot be so difficult to simply open a door and look out into the corridor. She breathes in and out a couple of times, still undecided. She has never had anyone knock at the door before, and all officials know the regulations. Perhaps it is someone from another sector? It could even be someone who has been sent to floor thirty-six to test her.

She almost sits down again. If this is a test, she cannot afford to fail.

There is a louder knock at the door, and then the door opens and the large, uniform-clad security officer bursts into the room. He is holding on to a well-built man in a light-coloured zip-up jacket whose hands are cuffed in front of him. One of the man's eyes is red and is already swelling; he is also bleeding from a cut on his cheek. Both men are somewhat dishevelled.

The security officer straightens his uniform, taps in a message on his communication device, and strides over to the desk where the receptionist is sitting, trying to regain her former composure.

'A 630,' he says. 'Not the best way to finish a shift.' He sighs, and then says, 'You could've lent a hand; he's a burly bugger.'

The receptionist nods her head, thinking that 630 is code for illegal building access. She is also thinking that, given the 630's appearance, she would not have been much help.

The security officer, now somewhat calmer, is

obviously thinking the same. He looks at the receptionist and says with a short laugh, 'Though I doubt that there'd have been much *you* could've done.'

She shrugs. 'You know the regulations,' she says. Then she continues, wondering, 'How did he get in?'

The security officer, his eye on the man now standing quietly near the wall, says, 'Not sure. My guess is that he came up in the lift with your last customer. Difficult to do with all the cameras, but not impossible, and then he must have hidden in the toilet. Not sure why, though; why would anyone want to come up to floor thirty-six? What's here, besides the waiting room and—' He points towards the door at the front of the room.

The receptionist looks across at the man standing near the wall and thinks that they could always ask him.

She breathes a sigh of relief that everything has resolved itself so simply. It could have been worse; in fact, it could have been *much* worse if she had had to go out in to the corridor. Nothing happened; everything is still as it was. While thinking about how lucky she has been, she notes that her device is flashing, and, looking at the next paper, she calls out the number. There is no response, and in a slightly louder voice she calls out, '3325-678 to the door immediately.'

As she calls out the number, she realizes that it belongs to the girl with the green coat. She watches for a moment while the girl stands up hesitantly, looking at nothing in particular.

At the same time, two security officers enter the waiting room through the entry door, and, after quickly looking around the room, immediately move towards the first security officer who is now standing next to the 630. The three officers talk quietly among themselves for a few moments, more or less ignoring the man with the closed-up eye and the bloody face.

The receptionist watches them disinterestedly, not being able to catch everything that they are saying, and then picks up her knitting. She thinks: it will be good to have the girl with the green coat out of the waiting room; she has had an upsetting and unnerving effect on her.

The three security officers and the 630 begin to walk towards the exit door, and, forgetting her knitting, the receptionist watches them, still wondering why the man would have gone to all the trouble of getting himself to floor thirty-six and what he had wanted to do there. She watches the man, now walking between two of the officers, and speculates as to what will happen to him on the other side. Her eyes move over his clothes, which are fairly ordinary, and she notices that he is favouring one leg – perhaps a result of the fight with the officer. At the same time, a small part of her brain is thinking about her knitting, trying to remember where she was up to in her pattern.

Then, without any warning, she becomes aware of a

sound and a movement in front of her. She moves her attention from the men, now disappearing through the door, just in time to see the bag vanishing from her desk. Her senses begin to spring back into action as she becomes vividly aware of what is happening. The girl is hugging the bag and is now running across the room towards the exit door.

For a split second, she sits where she is as though glued to the spot, unable to move, and then she suddenly sees the situation in horrifying slow motion. She stands up, her chair skidding across the floor behind her, her knitting falling to the floor, and rushes across the room, screaming, 'Stop! I said *stop*. Stay where you are! You may not take the—'

But it is too late. The girl with the green coat opens the door and steps out of the room.

The door slams shut behind her.

There is an eerie quiet in the room. The three remaining people understand that something awful must have happened, even though they are not quite sure how to define what it is that is so awful: Surely there was nothing wrong with the girl wanting her bag back? It was rather unnecessary that the receptionist took it in the first place.

The bit about no personal belongings makes little sense and needs to be removed from the list of requirements. Perhaps the girl broke with regulations by taking the bag without asking, but then again it *was* her bag, and taking it can hardly be equated with the end of the world.

The receptionist's behaviour, however, makes them feel that perhaps it *is* the end of the world, and this, in turn, is making them extremely nervous.

A man in a three-piece suit stands up and, turning around, peers at the receptionist who has now returned to her desk. He appears to be about to say something, but although he opens his mouth he then hesitates, straightens his coat, and sits back down. An expression of under-standing - or is it pity? - slides across the face of a woman sitting a few seats away from him, and then she concentrates on her hands, lying in her lap.

For a moment the receptionist sits without moving, her knitting on her desk, her hands in her lap, not doing anything, completely overcome by the events of the past few minutes, then she takes several deep breaths, tidies the two piles of papers on her desk, and repositions her pen and her communication device. In the process, she knocks her knitting on the floor, yet again, and, when she retrieves it, she finds that a couple of stitches have fallen off the needle. She stifles an irritated exclamation and spends several minutes coaxing back the errant stitches.

Her hands are shaking while her mind, taking no pity

on her situation, insists on bringing up images of all the things that have gone wrong in one afternoon. She is relieved when her communication device flashes and she can call the next number.

Later, back in her unit, the receptionist relives those few panicked seconds between seeing the woman running for the door, with her bag clutched to her chest, and finally reacting. She can still hear herself screaming, knowing all the while that her screams were not going to change anything - the girl had already reached the exit door. It is as though it is a film being run on some kind of circular transmission: the same few seconds appear again and again and again.

Was there anything she could have done differently? She should never have left the bag on her desk; she could have placed it on the floor under the desk, or she could have called security and had it removed from the waiting room altogether. That is what she should have done. That is what *they* will tell her she should have done. 'Under no circumstance is anyone to have personal effects with them. In situations where this rule is disregarded, the effects should be removed forthwith from the room.' That is what they will say to her, and what they will mean is that everything that happened was all her fault. 3325-678 was not supposed to leave the waiting room with her bag: it is of utmost importance for the smooth running of the operation that everyone adheres to the regulations.

She prepares her dinner, but she eats very little. Sitting in the living room with a now cold cup of tea, her mind keeps returning to the waiting room and what she did or did not do, and what she could have or should have done. Right from the beginning, she had had a very strong feeling that 3325-678 was no good: she should have been keeping a very close eye on her - all the time. And, then, of course, there was that other woman; the one who screamed and had to be physically removed. 'No emotional outbursts,' they had said. What did they know about stressed people in waiting rooms?

She cannot relax; she sits on the edge of the chair as though she is preparing to take flight. In her head she is both the lawyer for the prosecution and the lawyer for the defence - she has given more than twenty years to Unitas; she has never made a mistake before; she should have been more vigilant. She should definitely have thought things through much better than she had.

The receptionist shakes her head, takes a sip of the cold tea, and, with the cup and saucer in her hands, walks to the kitchen. She tips out the unpalatable tea and begins to boil some more water. She needs to be doing things; she needs to be concentrating on practical, unimportant things that have nothing at all to do with waiting rooms or Unitas.

Surely they will be understanding.

There is a loud knock at the door. The sound terrifies her - it brings back the events of the evening - but she also knows that whoever is knocking must have priority access to the building; in fact, whoever it is would probably even have access to her unit. The knocking is simply someone in charge being polite.

The knocking comes again, and she turns off the kettle and walks to the door. She is feeling completely hollow inside; her feet are moving towards the door simply because something in her brain is telling them that they must, but inside of her a need to flee is growing exponentially. It has already filled her brain and her head and her entire body, and now it is threatening to burst out and fill the room.

There is nowhere to flee.

She opens the door.

Outside, in the corridor, there are two men. There is no one else in the corridor, and the space, which is normally quite large, seems to have receded, leaving only them. The receptionist does not recognize either of the men, but she can tell from their dark blue uniforms that they are Administration officials. One of them, large and red-faced, is carrying a small communication device and is obviously the person with most authority. The other one - younger and much fitter - is standing a couple of steps behind his colleague, and the receptionist guesses that he could be still learning the job.

More than anything she wants to close the door and retreat into her flat; she wants to believe that the men standing in front of her are simply some kind of mirage. She wants the mirage to disappear, and she wants every-thing to be as it was before - before the girl ran through the door with her awful bag, before the overweight woman began screaming, before the commotion in the corridor. Perhaps she would even like things to be as they were before Walter left her.

But she thinks: nothing is ever the way we believe it to be. We grab on to everything around us and we create our own realities. She wanted Walter to like her; she wanted to be seen as someone who was ordinary, accepted, even slightly popular. When Walter began to pay her attention, she built on his words and his actions, and she wove her own tapestry with herself at the centre. When he suddenly walked away she had to reconstruct her tapestry - she was still at its centre, but the images around her were different.

Standing in her hall, being confronted by two uniformed men, she knows that what she is seeing and feeling and interpreting is not the same as that which either of the men is seeing or experiencing. Everyone is in a cocoon of his or her own making, she thinks, while wondering how she might be able to remove herself and her cocoon somewhere else.

The man with the communication device steps through the door. His companion gives the receptionist a fleeting look as though he would like to apologize but has no idea what to say or where to begin. He nods at her as politely as is possible in the circumstances and follows his companion into the unit.

The receptionist wonders if she should invite them to sit down. Should she suggest tea, coffee? Should she concentrate on turning herself into a house spider and then crawl away into some corner before either of the men have noticed?

She shows the men into the living room, but neither of them sit. She decides that hot drinks are probably not going to be necessary.

The larger of the two men says, 'We are aware that it's late, 8733-110.' He glances down at his communications device and then looks straight at the receptionist. 'But management is disappointed,' he continues without removing his eyes from her face.

The receptionist returns the look. He is younger than she is; he was probably a pimply adolescent at the time of the Change. She is irritated that someone who was barely out of nappies when Unitas came to power is telling her that 'management is disappointed'. She was one of the forerunners; she was there when Unitas was still only an idea. She would like to tell him to leave, but she has always been cautious of anything to do with Administration, especially of late. Things have changed, people have changed, even the rules and regulations have changed. She knows too well what can happen when Administration takes a dislike to someone.

She suppresses her irritation and says, 'I can explain. It was not— '

'Most disappointed,' he continues, as though he has not even heard her speak.

His colleague moves his weight from one foot to the other and studies the barely noticeable patterns in the timber floor.

There is no point in concealing her irritation and trying to be civil. Being socially pleasant is not one of her major attributes, and she decides that she will probably make more headway being herself. In an attempt to fill her body with some kind of calm, she breathes in, feeling the air filling her lungs, holds her breath for a moment and enters a place where she is neither alive nor dead; then she breathes out. The large man in front of her is still talking, but she is no longer listening. She has travelled back-wards, and somewhere close by she is aware of Walter. In her mind she turns to face him. He is talking to her, but she is unable to catch all the words. She is straddled between several different tapestries, all of them with herself at the centre. She wonders why she has been thinking so much about Walter when she has not given him a thought in years.

She had always been 'different'. Before Walter, she had been what many would have called introverted or a loner; even now she can see herself back then, somewhere on the edge of everyone else. Was her silence all those years ago because she was waiting to be asked to speak, or was she simply listening and assessing the situation? Was she terrified of saying or doing the wrong thing, or for doing or saying something that could be interpreted as wrong? *Wrong* could have labelled her as someone whom no one really wanted to know; someone who did not fit in, and perhaps she realized that it was easiest and safest to keep quiet and remain in the background. Thinking back, she does not believe that she has ever been concerned about fitting in or saying or doing things that could be interpreted as being wrong - she has always been the person she is, someone on the outside, looking in.

But then she met Walter, and things changed.

She wonders if Walter had ever felt that she did not fit in, and whether he may have taken pity on her, realizing that she was different. Though it really does not make much difference now, or even then, after he had left her.

Going back in time, searching out her many other selves and the stories behind the selves seems to be helping her: the irritation and the fear of Administration is still there, but she is feeling slightly more in control, more herself.

The man doing all the talking is looking at her; obviously he is waiting for an answer, but she has not been listening. She has not heard what he has been saying.

'I'm sorry,' she begins, but then she thinks that she is not at all sorry and that she is sending the wrong message. She looks severely at the man, knowing that she needs to put him in his place.

'As you are already well aware, it has been a difficult day, and I am very tired - you said yourself that it is late. Management may well be disappointed, but I can assure you that it is not easy having to deal with hysterical women and people who think that they have a mind of their own. I am, after all, only the receptionist.'

It is obvious that this was not the answer the man was expecting, and for a moment he appears a little off-balance.

'So, if that's all, I'll thank you to leave now.' She is already walking towards the door, indicating that the two men are to do the same.

The man who has been studying the floor looks both relieved and thankful that the visit is almost at an end; he begins leaning towards the receptionist who is already at the front door.

His companion is not quite so thankful. Something has obviously gone wrong somewhere - he should be the person ending the conversation. He says, 'Just one moment, 8733-110.'

The receptionist, now standing with her hand on the door, turns her head very slightly and looks at him. 'Yes?' she says, while she thinks that this is just a new tapestry, and its finished appearance is completely up to her. Her fear of Administration is very real, but she understands, with sharp-edged clarity, that this fear does not have to be the focus of her reality. Her reality, which can only be now, this very moment, this instant, is all she has. This is who she is, standing in her hall, her hand close to the door panel, facing two uniformed Administration officials. All her other realities, tapestries, and experiences - even Walter - have been pulled together, diluted, reformed, translated, and packaged together into this moment.

She is acutely aware of her physical relationship to the two men - the three of them standing like chess pieces on a chessboard - in the same way as she is aware of the small, rectangular, stainless-steel door panel and the stillness of the living room behind the men. As far as she is concerned, the men in front of her are intruders, breaking strands in her perfect tapestry, clashing with all the creams and greys. She does not want to be drawn into their realities; she does not need to see anything the way they see it.

Despite her seemingly uncaring demeanour, the receptionist has often wondered about how other people experience the waiting room. She has plenty of time to think about such things, sitting in the same room day in and day out. She has never asked anyone if they like the white walls and the white panelled door, in the same way she has never discussed the appearance of her melamine desk. She firmly believes that no one sees anything in exactly the same way as anyone else, and it is the way we perceive things that dictates our reality.

She is aware that everyone has labelled her as uncaring and without empathy, but she would never have been able to do her job if she worried too much about what people were thinking or feeling. After Walter, she learnt that it was relatively easy to hide her feelings: feelings simply got in the way - they caused upset and disappointment. It was best to disassociate oneself from them.

The man with the communications device waves it in the air as he says, 'Don't worry about your shift tomorrow. You are to report to the Department of Administration and Justice, fifteenth floor, at ten o'clock.' A look of triumph washes over his face as he imparts his message. He steals a quick glance at his younger companion, wanting to share his moment of victory.

The receptionist smiles at him as she opens the door.

'I'll be there,' she says. 'I'm sure that we'll have a number of interesting things to talk about.' Inside, she is in turmoil. Nothing like this has ever happened to her before, and she is not sure that it is going to end happily.

EPILOGUE

Arthur is not dead; in fact, he is very much alive and, apart from the few aches and pains that come with age, is in reasonably good health. It is ten years since he was called to the waiting room, and he is a little hazy about what really happened there. He remembers that he had been extremely anxious and worried, and that his imagination had been running away with him: he truly believed that he was going to die. Looking back on it from the distance and safety of those ten extra years, he smiles condescendingly, seeing himself as someone else - someone who was a little confused, naïve even.

He forces his mind to return to the waiting room and to the moment before he left by the door at the front of the room. He remembers that he had been worrying about what was on the other side, and, thinking back, he believes that he may have imagined a line of torturers or a black void into which he expected he would fall or be pushed. He is quite sure that it was the not knowing what was about to happen that had been stressing him out, and he remembers, standing at the front of the room, his hand on the door, uncertain whether he was fully prepared to take such a step into the unknown.

As his memory becomes clearer, he recalls how, when the door closed behind him, he was amazed to find himself in a large, but very ordinary, space. It was about the same size as the waiting room he had just left, but it could hardly be called a room, because on three sides it disappeared into wide corridors. In the centre of the space there was a wide screen suspended from the ceiling, and on the screen he could see his number, 7891-447, flashing. At the same time he noticed a red light above the corridor on his right, flashing with the same frequency. Something told him that there was a connection between the flashing number and the light, and he began to move to the right.

It was a relatively short corridor that ended in a very large, airy room divided on one side into many small cubicles. There was a lively buzz from people talking, moving around, and using a variety of screens and computing consoles. After the relative silence and heaviness of the waiting room, it all came as a pleasant change, and as Arthur entered the room, a man came forward, a small PS in his hand.

'7891-447?' he asked, looking quite confident that the man in front of him *was* 7891-447.

Arthur nodded.

The man indicated one of the cubicles. 'They're waiting for you.'

Although Arthur certainly did not like the sound of the plural pronoun and all it might contain, he gave the man something that resembled a smile and entered the cubicle.

The cubicle was not particularly large nor was it overly small, and the walls, which did not reach the ceiling, managed to give the necessary amount of privacy from the cubicles on either side. There was a plain desk - made from some kind of synthetic material - three padded chairs, one of them behind the desk, and a sleek, black PS - the only thing that was visible on the desk. There were no pictures or posters on the walls, and the room had a clean, but austere, feel about it.

Arthur hastily noted the man behind the desk and the man seated on one of the two chairs in front of the desk. Despite the compactness of the room, the second man was partially in shadow, possibly because he was seated with his back to the door.

He did not turn around when Arthur entered.

Not sure what to do next, Arthur approached the desk as the tired-looking man behind the desk waved him to the empty chair.

'7891-447, please sit down. We must apologize for the long delay, but it was completely out of our hands.' The sketchiest of smiles crossed his face as he continued, 'It was your brother's fault, actually.' He looked pointedly at the man sitting in the other chair. 'He was to have been here at four, but, well... ' his voice faded off as his attention was captured by the expression on Arthur's face.

Arthur had been about to sit down when he heard the words *your brother*, and he remained in a half-sitting pose, unsure if had heard correctly.

The man who had been sitting now stood up and faced Arthur. He hesitated for a moment before reaching over and giving him an untidy hug.

They made it sound as though it had all been Arthur's fault: he had simply not wanted to be reunited with his family. They claimed that they had been working towards this reunion for years. The man behind the desk showed him several screens, all covered with the text that, according to him, was confirmation that they had spent a lot of time trying to bring about a successful reunion.

Arthur sat down. He was in a state of shock: he had been about to be killed, executed most horribly - or so he thought - and here he was in a normal, busy office space for the sole purpose of being reunited with his brother whom he had not seen for two decades. He wondered briefly if this could simply be part of some psychological form of torture. Perhaps the person who claimed to be George was not real; perhaps the person behind the desk was not real either. For all Arthur knew, the two of them - and the room as well, for that matter - could be some kind of hologram, and once Arthur accepted that the man next to him really *was* his brother, then everything would disappear. He looked around hesitantly: he did not want to be fooled, but, on the other hand, he could not let go of the possibility that the man sitting only centimetres from him really might be his brother.

The man behind the desk asked him if he would like tea or coffee, and Arthur, thinking back to the hours in the waiting room with nothing to drink but water from a tap in the toilet, said he would have coffee. He remembered how, only recently, he had meditated on coffee; its smell, its flavour, its rounded warmth.

Coffee in small blue coffee cups on blue saucers, with cream and sugar on the side, and a plate of elongated shortbread biscuits soon arrived on a white tray carried into the cubicle by a young man dressed in black. The man behind the desk nodded at him, and the young man, having placed the tray on the desk, quietly left the room.

Arthur closed his eyes and breathed in the strong, aromatic smell of the coffee. If this was all a hologram then it was amazingly clever. Perhaps the person who called himself his brother *was* his brother after all. He half-turned and looked at him as he savoured that very first sip of the hot liquid. Mentally adding fifteen, twenty years to the image of George that he had carried with him all those years, he had to admit that the man seated next to him was very like the man he remembered as being his brother.

The man behind the desk was talking and was telling him how much everyone had looked forward to this reunion. His finger was bringing up the different screens on his PS. 'We had almost given up,' he said, looking directly at Arthur.

Arthur was confused, greatly confused. He put down his half-empty cup on the saucer and said, 'But the letters? I wrote so many letters.'

The man behind the desk shook his head.

George joined in. 'There were no letters, Arthur.' Arthur inwardly froze, hearing his name: people did not use names. He glanced at his brother and at the man behind the desk, but neither of them looked as though there was anything out of place. 'We didn't receive any letters,' George said, looking directly at the man behind the desk who shook his head a second time.

Arthur shrugged. He thought of all the letters and other communications he had written over the years - that is, before he eventually gave up. He thought of the way he had been treated by the different departments. He had been ignored, snubbed, even ridiculed.

A worrying thought surged to the front of his mind. Is it possible that he had only imagined writing the letters? Perhaps he had thought about writing letters, but he had never sent them, and perhaps that was the reason the authorities had ridiculed him. Perhaps everyone else - the authorities, the man behind the desk and even his brother - were right when they said that there were no letters, and he is wrong.

He drank the rest of his coffee and listened while the man behind the desk explained how Arthur's brother - 9683-725 - (so that is his number, thought Arthur) had contacted the Department of Administration and Justice a year or so ago, hoping to be reunited with his brother. The process was lengthy (this did not surprise Arthur at all) - 'personal privacy must be retained at all costs,' added the man behind the desk.

'Of course, we always knew where you were,' the man said, 'but we had to consider that you might not want to be reunited with your brother; we had to respect this possibility.'

Arthur felt that the whole meeting or interview or whatever one might want to call it was descending into surreality. He wondered whether his brother felt the same or whether he found the whole situation completely normal.

If they knew where he was, why had they taken so long to contact him? He could understand the bit about personal privacy, but all they had needed to do was to ask.

Perhaps his perception and understanding of what was going on around him was all wrong, simply because it had been a very long, frustrating day and he was so tired. Perhaps he was muddling up facts with what he suspected or believed to be true. All he really wanted was to go home and go to bed. He would also like to be able to talk to his brother without anyone else around. He was still trying to assimilate the fact that his brother - his own real-life brother - was sitting next to him. Arthur had given up on seeing him years ago - George had been relegated to that part of his memory that housed memories of his grandparents and his parents. Now he was sitting next to him, and it was taking Arthur time to remove him from his memory and into the present.

Not for a moment did he believe the man behind the desk and his talk about there being no letters; nor did he believe that they were reluctant to approach him because of privacy concerns. Obviously someone had blundered, and now they were trying to smooth it over the best they could.

Arthur never found out what had indeed happened: if someone had been at fault, if it had simply been a misunderstanding, or if it had been something more sinister. He did find out, however, that George had done particularly well for himself, career-wise.

From what Arthur could piece together, George had first worked as an accountant - he was studying accountancy when he disappeared - and then auditor for several years before becoming chief financial officer in the sector where he was then living. At this point the Party had obviously noted his potential, and he was moved sideways into the office of the Minister for Finance. Within a few years, he had managed to leapfrog all the other aspirants in the ministry to become the Assistant Minister for Finance. It was at this point that George realized that he could use his position to reconnect with his brother.

George was amazed that Arthur believed that it was he and his parents who had disappeared, when all the time it was they who had been wondering what had happened to Arthur.

Later, when they were no longer anywhere near Building C, Arthur tried to explain to George that he had been in the kitchen with their parents the day that they had been taken away, but George simply shook his head and said that Arthur had been confused - no one had been taken away. It did not seem to matter how Arthur described what had happened, his brother simply discarded it as the result of an overly active imagination.

Arthur was quite sure that his imagination had nothing at all to do with it.

He learnt that, sadly, his father had passed away some years earlier, but his mother was still living, in the same sector as George. When Arthur finally met her some weeks later, she reminded Arthur outwardly of the woman whom he remembered as his mother, but she was suffering from a form of dementia, and any chance of them renewing contact with each other had completely disappeared.

Sometimes he felt that it was probably best so. It had been too difficult, trying to explain something that even he did not fully understand. She seemed to recognize him at times, and in her mind at least he felt that he had always been part of her reality.

He was moved to a tower block in the same sector as his brother, and he thought about the dream he had - was it a dream? - where he had seen someone who resembled his brother. Dreams and reality are now intertwined: he is no longer sure what is real and what might be something that he is simply imagining. There are lots of other people living in his tower block, and there are also efficient-looking people in white coats: people who Arthur understands are there to help and assist. One of them brings him small green and pink pills every morning and evening, while another accompanies him of an afternoon when he takes a walk around the gardens.

He is no longer working. They told him that there are no positions available at the moment but that they will notify him as soon as something becomes available. He does not mind: he is content. He plays chess and occasionally he sees George.

Perhaps Unitas is not so bad after all.

Thea stands on the other side of the door for a few moments, clutching her bag. She is amazed that she managed to retrieve the bag, and for the first time in more than two hours she feels somewhat calm and collected, and even slightly confident. The door has closed behind her, but she has still not fully taken in her surroundings; she is far too occupied absorbing the fact that she is now on the other side of the door and that she has her bag with her. Finally, she moves her bag on to her shoulder and takes a look at where she is standing.

Nothing is the way she imagined it.

She is in what appears to be a long corridor, and, standing a little to her left, there is a man in a dark blue uniform. She winces, thinking that he has probably been there since she came through the door and that he has most probably been standing there, watching her.

The man says, '3325-678? This way, please.'

Thea nods her head and follows the man along the corridor. There is no one else to be seen. She considers asking him where they are going, but decides that she will find out soon enough and that it is unlikely that her guide will give her any information in advance.

She guesses that the corridor is like all other corridors in the building, assuming, of course, that they are still in the same building. The floors are timber and the walls are off-white. She reflects for a moment on the fact that she has not seen all the corridors in the building, but she dismisses the thought as irrelevant: in all probability the corridors are all exactly the same.

As with the previous corridor, her shoes make a soft smacking sound as they connect with the smooth timber of the flooring, and she finds herself hurrying in order to keep up with the uniformed official. At the end of the corridor they enter a large lift.

Whether they descend one floor or ten floors is impossible for Thea to judge - all lifts move so quickly - but when the lift stops and the doors glide back, they are facing a large, brightly lit space, at the far end of which there are three doors, obviously leading to three separate rooms.

As far as Thea can see, there is no one around.

As they exit the lift, Thea turns to the official and asks

quietly, 'Is this the Medical Centre?', knowing that it looks nothing like a medical centre and wondering where the man has taken her.

He frowns and shakes his head.

'But my shoulder? That's why I'm here, isn't it?'

He looks puzzled and puts together the longest sentence he has spoken since they met. 'Your shoulder? This has absolutely nothing to do with your shoulder.'

A coldness moves through her body, surging out to her very fingertips. She remembers how the lack of a letterhead has been worrying her since she first received the letter, and how she has tried to tell herself that someone had simply made a mistake. She thinks back to Aaron and the fact that he has disappeared and that there must be many unanswered questions to which someone, somewhere, most probably wants answers.

She does not say anything, because she knows that there is nothing she can say, and, to be perfectly honest, she is unable to speak. She simply bites her lip and nods her head as if in agreement - *this has absolutely nothing to do with my shoulder,* she thinks.

Her guide indicates that she is expected at the third room, the one on the far right, then his communication device blinks, and he turns and walks back to the lift.

Thea thinks back to the waiting room and to the medical centre that she imagined she visited. Images of the nurse with the drink that could have been orange but was probably something else, the little round doctor, and the secretary flood back over her. She remembers how her bag was not present in some of her fantasies while it was there in others. She remembers the tall man with the glasses, and how no one had seen him - though, of course, the people in the medical centre were part of her imaginings, they were not part of the real world.

But what is real and what is simply the result of some fantasy or dream? She has never thought like this before; her head feels like a spinning top as she considers the possibility that, in the same way as the medical centre was not real, what is going on at the moment may not necessarily be real. She is no longer sure what she means by *real*.

She quickly scans the space and at the three closed doors on the far side. There is not a sound anywhere, but she imagines that behind each of those closed doors there is someone waiting. Waiting for what?

Are they waiting for her?

Aaron's description of his interview is still very much at the front of her brain, but then she thinks that that was *his* experience - or what he thought was his experience - filtered through his own unique collection of perspectives and his own likes and dislikes. Perhaps it was not that bad after all; or perhaps it was much, much worse.

She feels as though she is rushing through the cosmos, and there is nothing to hold on to. She grabs the strap of her bag and leans against the wall. If there are people in the space, they are all hidden behind the three doors, and someone in the third room is waiting for her to push open the door.

She does not have a lot of time, and she must decide what to do.

The lift door opens easily, in spite of her concern that it would not; once in the lift, she activates the button for the ground floor and then holds her breath. There are no loud warning signals and no flashing red lights indicating an error. The lift drops obediently through the building, and the doors slide open as it comes to rest.

Thea steps out of the lift.

Beyond the glass windows of the building, it is dark outside, and, although she cannot see through the windows, she is almost certain that there are people hurrying along the street. The foyer itself is almost empty, except for a couple of people sitting on a lounge at the far end, and a noisy group of office workers congregated near the entry.

Suddenly everything feels normal again. Not completely normal but almost.

She walks out of the building. The cool evening air rushes against her face, and she breathes in deeply. She feels strangely light and free; it is almost as though she has been released from prison, and now she has her whole life in front of her.

She has already walked past several buildings before she begins to wonder where she should go. She could go home, but something is pulling her in another direction.

Outside Aaron's house, she stops for a few moments before lifting the latch to the gate and walking down the stone path. She knows that she is doing the right thing, and her steps are confident. When she reaches the door, she knocks and then steps back and waits.

Aaron opens the door. He is smiling as he invites her in and closes the door behind her. He says, 'It all has to do with perspective. I knew that you would understand, eventually.'

As they walk down the hall he asks her, 'Tea or coffee?'

Once the receptionist has closed the door behind the two Administration officials, she stands in the hall for a moment, grateful for the quietness and the emptiness of her unit, while her mind continues to churn through what they had told her: *'You are to report to the Department of Administration and Justice, fifteenth floor, at ten o'clock.'*

It has not come as a surprise: she knows that everyone in Unitas, except for the people right at the very top, is completely expendable. People are recruited, and when it becomes obvious that they no longer have anything to give the Party, they are asked to leave. Or, as is often the case, they are pushed; either way, the result is the same. She has reached the end of her usefulness, and as far as she can see, there is only one thing left for her to do.

She checks the time on her screen and sees that at the

most she has twelve hours to do what she has to do. She is almost certain that there are still no remarks against her number - access and benefits will only be curtailed after her impending ten o'clock meeting at the Department of Administration and Justice.

Now that she has decided on a plan of action, she feels calmer and more in control. She hurriedly puts a few things into an orange backpack and then walks quickly around the unit, checking the lights, the placement of chairs, the cover on her bed, towels in the bathroom... She places the black bag with her knitting into a large wardrobe, but not before she slips her PS into her backpack. She sits on the side of her bed, trying to think of something she may have missed, before retrieving the PS, opening a screen and typing in a code. The numbers take her to yet another screen where she is told that only people with authority will be able to proceed. She types in a fifteen-digit number and breathes a sigh of relief when the code is accepted and she recognizes the new screen. When prompted, she types in her own number and activates a twenty-four hour non-surveillance option. Eventually, she will be asked to explain her reasons for taking such a liberty, but that is not her biggest concern at the moment. Although it is unlikely that anyone would have thought to track her movements before the meeting with the Department of Administration and Justice, she is not prepared to take any unnecessary risks. As she returns the PS to the backpack, she is thankful for the few small advantages she has as receptionist.

Then, after taking one last look around the rooms, she dims the lights, takes her grey coat from the coat-rack in the hall, and steps out into the corridor.

She knows exactly where she has to go and what she has to do, and she realizes why she has been thinking of Walter so much during the day. It is almost as though he is there next to her, trying to tell her something. Perhaps he did care after all. Perhaps he has cared all the time, but she was blinded by all the things around her and did not understand. Now, finally, she believes that she understands.

It is a short walk to the train station, and a quick glance at the huge electronic screen shows that she has only ten minutes to wait for her train. She is relieved; she does not want to have to endure empty hours when she might begin to question what she is about to do, or, even worse, change her mind.

She sits down on a polished brown bench on the ultra-clean platform and watches the few people who are waiting for the same train. She does not expect to know any of them, and she is comfortably certain that none of them could possibly know who she is. A warm feeling of satisfaction courses through her body, and she smiles at a woman walking past.

On the train, after the uniformed train official has checked everyone's PB, the receptionist fetches a coffee from the coffee machine. Given her present situation, she is strangely calm, and she wonders if it may have something to do with the fact that she now feels in control. She looks out at the impenetrable darkness beyond the window and considers if she has ever felt as much in control as she does at that moment.

At some point she falls asleep; when, quite some time later, she jolts awake, she wonders where she is. She focuses and remembers that she is on a train, and gradually she remembers everything that has happened and what she is about to do. As her mind lurches back on track, she worries that she may have missed her station, and she anxiously checks the electronic trip guide above the door of her carriage. Relieved to see that she still has fifteen minutes before she is to reach her destination, she relaxes and lets her attention aimlessly drift. She can still not see anything beyond the window, only her reflection looking back at her.

The carriage is almost empty; when she alights at the next station, she and an elderly man are the only two people on the platform, but it is already well after midnight, so she is not particularly surprised.

She passes through the station gate to the outside,

feeling exhilarated by the cold mountain air rushing against her face. The elderly man has already disappeared down one of the many small streets, and the receptionist is completely on her own. The streets are empty, and there are no lights showing in any of the small houses.

She reflects that this is one of the areas where Administration has not yet managed to move everyone into high-rise accommodation. The area has been incorporated into at least two sectors, but most people have been allowed to remain in their own homes. Superficially, very little has changed.

The realization propels her back into the past, and without thinking she searches for Walter. She pulls herself together and begins walking along the dimly lit road. There is a soft, cold mist wrapping itself around everything, and she thinks: Yes, this is how it should be; this is how it would have been all those years ago.

As she turns off the main road and heads up the steep hill, she is almost certain that Walter is walking a few steps behind her. On her left, beyond the narrow strip of dark trees and bushes, she knows that the mountain falls away into the valley and that beyond that valley there are more mountains and more valleys.

She is surprised that the walk uphill is tiring her, but she has worked all afternoon and evening, and now it is close to two in the morning. It is only the knowledge of what she has to do that keeps her going, step after step.

The mist is getting thicker and, if possible, colder, and she pulls her coat close around her. She is thankful that she remembered to bring her coat; she would have been very cold without it.

At the top of the hill, the road curves out towards the side of the mountain, creating a small paved viewing area.

Without turning her head, she says: 'Is this one of the places we would have visited, Walter?' and she is almost certain that he answers in the affirmative.

She nods, as if in answer, and walks to the edge of the viewing area. It may be dark, but there is a full moon, and she can see across the valley to the mountains in the distance. As she looks across the vast expanse of wilderness, she reflects that, in parts, it is almost two thousand metres to the valley below. She leans over the low fence, trying to understand what two thousand metres looks like, but, in spite of the moon, shadows and long fingers of darkness intersect with the mist, making it difficult for her to see anything clearly.

She sits on the fence, her back to the view, her coat pulled up around her ears. Then she takes off her backpack, places it on the ground so that it is next to her, leaning against the fence, and opens it. Her fingers are cold, and she blows on them for a few moments before rummaging in the bag. The thought runs through her head that she should have worn gloves.

From the bottom of the bag, she pulls out her black

pen with the gold trim, the one she received for ten years' service. She holds it in her hand briefly, enjoying the smoothness, and then, half-turning towards the drop, throws it as far as she can.

Next she pulls out her PS; standing up and turning around, she lets the PS follow the pen.

'You were right,' she says. 'It was the wrong way. I should have listened to you; I should have understood, but I didn't.' Like an echo she adds, 'I didn't listen, and I didn't understand.'

It looks as though she could be talking with someone standing next to her. Is there really someone standing there? Only she would know.

'I'm sorry, Walter. I know I blamed you, but now I understand. It was Unitas, wasn't it? Unitas came between us without my even realizing. The whole can never be better than its parts; I know that now. A society that ignores the individual is doomed to fail.'

She pauses for a moment, and then she says, 'Perhaps not today, not even tomorrow, but eventually.'

She steps over the fence and looks down at the drop beneath her feet. 'Sitting in that waiting room, day after day, week after week, I became someone I did not want to be. I slotted into their idea of the whole, and I lost myself. My outlook on everything, my way of thinking, changed. I became bitter. I lost myself, Walter, but all of that is about to change.'

Her feet are on a ledge jutting out from the side of the mountain; below her, there is a shadowy space with surreally drawn vegetation loosely wrapped in long lengths of swirling mist. Without paying the thought very much attention, she feels that everything around her is like a scene from a black-and-white film. Above her is the moon, silent and non-judgemental.

She shivers a little. From the cold? From what she is about to do?

Is Walter still next to her? She is not sure, but she believes so.

'Things could have been so very different,' she says to no one in particular, as she closes her eyes, takes a deep breath, and steps out into the abyss.